Rock Big and Sing Loud

Rock Big
and Sing Loud

by
Tamara Baxter

*To Bonnie —
my new SELU
friend —*

*Tamara Baxter
SeLu 08*

Preface by
Phil Krummrich

Introduction by
Robert Morgan

Jesse Stuart Foundation
Ashland, Kentucky
2006

To my husband, Colin,
and son, Andrew

FIRST EDITION

ISBN: 1-931672-41-5

Published By:
Jesse Stuart Foundation
P.O. Box 669 • Ashland, KY 41105
(606) 326-1667 • JSFBOOKS.com

Contents

Acknowledgments

The author wishes to acknowledge the following literary journals and anthologies where several of these short stories appeared, and to the literary contests that awarded prizes.

Artemis: Jack Mooneyham Is Going to Hell
Frontage Road: A Wind Among the Stars
In-Place: An Anthology of Appalachian Writers: rpt. Jack Mooneyham is Going to Hell
Pine Mountain Sand and Gravel: Me and My Mean Sister Mary Lee
Mockingbird: Doomsday Monday at Pee Wee's Hamburger Emporium
Now & Then: Some Living Room
Nightshade Nightstand Reader: Where the Fishes Swim
O. Henry Awards Anthology 2000: Dustbusters
Tennessee Landscape: People and Places: Black Dark
Wellspring: Killing Oranges
Harriett Arnow Award: Dustbusters (1st prize)
Leslie Garrett Fiction Prize: To Boldly Go (3rd prize)
Mockingbird: Doomsday Monday at Pee Wee's Hamburger Emporium (1st prize)
Rose Post National Award for Creative Writing: Some Living Room (2nd prize)
Sherwood Anderson Award: Tizzie Dearstone's Night Lace (2nd prize)
Tennessee Mountain Writers' Award: Black Dark (1st prize)
Virginia Highlands Writers' Fiction Award for Short Fiction: Killing Oranges (1st prize)

Special Thanks

I am sincerely grateful to all the fine writers who taught me what I know about the craft of writing fiction, either in college classrooms or in the Appalachian Writers' Workshops at Hindman Settlement School, Hindman, Kentucky. These are Lee Smith, Robert Morgan, Gurney Norman, Lisa Alther, James Still, Lisa Koger, Meredith Sue Willis, Silas House, Joyce Dyer, Sharon McCrumb, Albert Stuart, and Robert J. Higgs. I am especially grateful to Radford University's SELU Writers' Retreat and to my SELU sisters and brothers, all acclaimed writers, with whom I have shared the writing life for nearly two decades. These are Parks Lanier, Isabel Zuber, Heidi Hartwiger, Darnell Arnoult, Bill Brown, Harry Dean, Dianne Jordan, and Jeanne Shannon.

A special thanks to Mrs. Katie Williams who suggested the title of this collection while telling me a family story.

A sincere thanks to Phil Krummrich and Chris Holbrook of Morehead State University for their assistance in the editing of the manuscript, and to the renowned Jesse Stuart Foundation that makes possible this collection of short stories, *Rock Big and Sing Loud*.

Preface

The Department of English, Foreign Languages, and Philosophy at Morehead State University, in partnership with the Jesse Stuart Foundation, is proud to inaugurate with this volume the New Writers Series. The Series reflects the mission of the University in several ways, and especially this goal: "improving the quality of life for the commonwealth in which we live and work, while protecting and preserving the unique history and heritage of our service region." We live and work in Morehead and in Kentucky, but also in Appalachia; protecting and preserving our history and heritage, in our view, also includes encouraging new expressions of that history and heritage. This is in perfect harmony with the mission of The Jesse Stuart Foundation, which "…is devoted to preserving the human and literary legacy of Jesse Stuart and other Kentucky and Appalachian writers," and which has as its primary purpose: "to produce books which supplement the educational system at all levels." On behalf of the department and the University, I would like to acknowledge and thank Dr. James M. Gifford, Secretary of the Jesse Stuart Foundation, and Mr. Keith R. Kappes, Chair of the Board of Directors, for their vision and support in developing this partnership and making this Series possible.

It is one of the ironies of our time that good publishing opportunities appear to be diminishing, even though there are more talented writers at work now than at any time in history. Appalachia produces remarkable numbers of fine storytellers and poets, and yet it has become harder than ever before for those authors to publish their work in book form. The New Writers Series will enable one deserving writer per year to realize the dream of a first book. We intend to alternate between fiction and poetry, and perhaps also creative non-fiction.

This year's winner was chosen by a committee made up of writers from Morehead State University and the community: Rebecca Bailey, George Eklund, Chris Holbrook, and Bob Sloan. I had the privilege of joining the group as an administrator. We were impressed by the high quality and rich diversity of the submissions, and we expect that several of the authors who submitted their work will go on to distinguish themselves. In the end, however, after much rereading and cordial debate, the committee chose *Rock Big and Sing Loud* by Tamara Baxter as the winning manuscript.

Ms. Baxter is from Tennessee, and her work shows that she has been listening keenly and watching closely her whole life. The 16 comic and tragic short stories in this collection take place in the fictionalized rural Southern Appalachian town and county of Dixon. Whether she lets the characters speak for themselves in first-person stories, or reports their experiences in third-person narratives, she captures their nuances convincingly. There is outrage in this collection: she protests against the brutality and deprivation and sheer bad luck that mar the lives of so many, particularly so many women and children. There is rich humor: the humor of a family member and neighbor, laughing at and with people she knows and loves. Above all, there is compassion: compassion for those not blessed with the full use of their minds, for those who have grown old, for those who are bewildered by the changing world around them, for those who are trying their best to contrive a happy life for themselves and the ones they love.

I will mention just a few of the stories here, so that you can get on with your reading. "Dustbusters" is a wickedly funny tale of the fortunes of the ashes of poor Peony Duggernaut. "Black Dark" and "Killing Oranges" present brave confrontations with abuse. In "Charlie," "To Boldly Go," and "A Wind Among the Stars," Baxter shows us the world from the point of view of people who are not all there, by society's usual standards. "The Resurrection of Hannah Belle Hogan" will make you want to stand up and cheer, or at least grin. As for "Doomsday Monday at Pee Wee's Hamburger Emporium" —no, I won't try to tell you, but I believe you'll enjoy it. Read *Rock Big and Sing Loud*. You will recognize the people and places, and you will come to understand them in new ways.

Phil Krummrich

Foreword

It is a pleasure and an honor to welcome and celebrate Tamara Baxter's story collection *Rock Big and Sing Loud*, winner of the Jesse Stuart Foundation First Author's Prize in Fiction. The award recognizes significant work by a new writer in the Southern Appalachian region. Named for the outstanding Kentucky author of fiction, poetry and nonfiction, Jesse Stuart, the prize calls attention to the virtual renaissance of exciting writing now produced in the area. The timing of this publication could not be better.

Anyone who reads this book of stories will be impressed by the strong sense of place, the mountains of eastern Tennessee, and the authenticity of the voices in both the dialogue and the narration. It is clear Baxter has absorbed the long-standing tradition of narrative writing that includes Harriette Arnow, author of *The Dollmaker*, Mildred Haun, author of *The Hawk's Done Gone*, as well as more recent fiction writers such as Lee Smith.

Baxter demonstrates perfect ear in capturing and rendering the talk of the region, whether spoken by poor folk or more affluent individuals. She draws on the colorful tradition of storytelling, the oral history, the tall tale, the comic hyperbole of the culture, and tells stories of sly humor and wry drama, taking unexpected turns, making surprising connections.

According to the Irish writer and critic Frank O'Connor in his study *The Lonely Voice*, the short story almost always portrays the outsider to society, the person of marginal consequence and power. Baxter brings to life in these pages the voices and lives of those long forgotten or ignored. She is especially successful in writing about the struggles of women, the pains and satisfactions of marriage in a world of ignorant, often violent men.

Baxter looks at the world of the rural past with her eyes wide open, offering no sentimental pieties or nostalgia. In "Dustbusters" she presents an angry widower who "hadn't got his mileage out of Peony."

In "Killing Oranges" an abused wife imagines driving a nail through her husband's ear, and does. In "Me and My Mean Sister" wicked little girls wreak catastrophe on neighbors and pretend innocence. Many are stories of women talking to women, talking to the reader, opening windows on confused but compelling lives.

Baxter shows an exact and detailed knowledge of the rural world, describing how seed corn is selected, how potatoes are planted, young puppies are killed, and how onion poultices are used for treating the sick. She writes poor black voices as well as poor white voices. But many of her best stories take place in the contemporary world also, in suburbs, in towns, in trailer parks. She writes vividly about a world of television talk shows, shopping malls, *Victoria's Secret* catalogs, *Star Trek*, and the vicissitudes of old age. In one of the very best stories, "To Boldly Go," the drunken husband Eddy, obsessed with *Star Trek* when fired from his job in a chicken factory, hears voices in frying pans and light fixtures, and imagines he is beamed aboard *The U.S.S. Enterprise* by Scotty.

In the unforgettable story "Flashpoint," a dying woman fights mentally for her husband's love with "the blond vulture" nurse who has been hired to take care of her. Baxter's best subject is marriage, and nowhere does she dramatize the struggles and pleasures of married love more effectively than in this short narrative. "You think he will change. He never does. He thinks you will always stay the same. You never can." In the end, though the wife loses both her husband and her life, she experiences an ultimate elation of freedom.

In "A Christmas Mourning" a young and foolish husband attempts to confront the death in childbirth of his very young wife. All he knows to do is mindlessly chop down chestnut tree after chestnut tree. The midwife, Granny Older, meditates on his confusion and rashness.

"A woman knew how to accept and go on better than a man. A woman knew to wait until the day closed, the children in bed asleep, the husband satisfied and snoring on his side, only the night sounds of crickets and creaking planks of the house to meditate on. This is the time of letting go of grief, sobbing so quietly and still no one hears her private sorrows spoken into her pillow, her hands clinching and un-clinching until she lets go of her heart and falls asleep."

Baxter knows how to reveal a character and a time and place

through one detail, a single sentence. In "Some Living Room" the elderly black man, Silas Mosely, who lives next door in a shed on a neighbor's farm, "sometimes sat on the porch and watched the *Amos and Andy* show through the side window." The multiple ironies evoked by that one image are awesome.

In the final story of the collection, "Rock Big and Sing Loud," we follow the thoughts of a woman nearly 106 years old as she plans her own death. "Orey toured the palace of her mind with fingers reading the Braille of the fireplace." She chooses the rocking chair on the porch as the place of her departure. "Dying was just like rocking back in time."

The past decade has been an exciting time for American fiction in general and Southern Appalachian fiction in particular. Tamara Baxter's stories are a significant addition to this surge of new writing. Her narratives can make you laugh or break your heart, and sometimes they do both at once. It is an important paradox that the most regionally specific fiction is also the most universally accessible. Almost all literary fiction is regional, even local, in its setting and idiom. It is the exactness of detail and voice, and depth of characterization, that make a story alive for readers everywhere.

Writing truly about the world of eastern Tennessee Baxter also writes about the world at large, about humanity. She has given us the stories of some of the most afflicted and addicted, the most failed and failing, individuals on the planet, and also some of the strongest and most enduring people we are ever likely to meet. These stories take us to places we did not expect to go, and just when we think we have seen what is strangest, most absurd, most alien and outrageous, we recognize something of ourselves.

Robert Morgan

Dustbusters

It's fitting that Peony Duggernaut is finally buried in a flower pot on sister Iris and sister Pansy's front stoop. Left side, third stoop up. Right in the middle. Right among the petunias and the geraniums. Gray ashes, silky as talcum powder, and chunks and bits of bone. Splintery pieces. That describes Peony when she was put in Iris's new blue flower pot, mixed up with topsoil, and sphagnum for draining, potted up and pressed down. The flowerpot was certainly a great improvement from where Peony was before, rusting in peace in an old tin can that her husband, Dingo Duggernaut, took her home in after the funeral.

Dingo wouldn't pay. He wouldn't have none of them fancy clay pots with the dome lids that seal down like a pickle jar. Mr. Minott, the mortician, poured Peony Duggernaut, still warm from the oven and smelling like hot field lime, into an old Karo Syrup tin he had on the shelf. One-gallon size. Real old. With old buttons and zippers and metal snaps his mama had saved for sewing and mending. Been on the shelf for years. You could see the yellow spot on the wallpaper when he took the tin down, dumped them buttons and zippers in the trash with one swish of his hand.

Anyway, Mr. Minott was give out arguing with Dingo Duggernaut on the subject of decency. Dingo said, "Damned if I'll lay out good money on Peony now she's dead, and I had not one cause to spend a penny on her living. Don't make no sense."

Iris maintained that the family had to get sister Peony buried proper. Get Peony out of the trunk of Dingo's old '64 Rambler where he'd been hauling her around since the undertaker sifted her ashes into the syrup tin. Pansy begged Dingo to behave with Christian decency. Begged him to put Peony to rest in a proper way. Decency to Dingo Duggernaut was setting Peony in the trunk of his Rambler with his toolbox, his fishing gear, and his hunting boots.

Iris and Pansy never did get along with Dingo. Sit on their front porch and visit for more than five minutes and Dingo's name will come up. "There's a lifetime of cheapness behind Dingo Duggernaut," Pansy always begins.

"And he's as crooked as he is cheap." Iris takes over Pansy's story. She throws her hands in the air. "Laws, Dingo's so crooked its grown on him like a sign. Stand back and study him awhile and you'll see."

That's the truth about Dingo for he's got a crooked grin that lays a-slash his face. His overalls hang crooked because his left shoulder drops down and his right shoulder is hitched up almost to his ear lobe. His hat rides off his head sideways. He's walleyed. He's pigeon-toed. Dingo's back is hunched. Makes his head swing toward the ground. Yes, Dingo's about as sigodlin a man as you'll ever meet.

"But his being crooked is no where the measure of how cheap and mean spirited Dingo Duggernaut can be," Pansy will tell you, rocking faster and faster as she gets her story wound up. "All them Duggernauts are that way."

There was some truth in that, too, for Dingo made Peony cook the pinto beans with the same soup bone ten times before he'd throw it to the dogs. Dingo broke up the kitchen chairs and burned them for stove kindling so Peony couldn't sit down and break the beans or peel a turnip. Dingo put boards under the mattress on Peony's side of the bed to make sure she didn't sleep too sound. Said he wouldn't have a lazy woman around the house.

"And never a day went by that Dingo Duggernaut didn't check the trash can to see what sister Peony might have thrown away. Dingo made her fish out the potato parings and hold them up to the window to make sure she had peeled them thin enough to see through," says Iris, wiping her face on a white lace handkerchief.

"If she didn't? Lord, lord." Pansy sucks her teeth and shakes her head whenever she hears Iris tell that story.

"Dingo Duggernaut is a heathen bound for hell," Iris brings her plump fist down on the arm of her rocker. She's counted the times on her fingers when she's heard Dingo say, "Nothing I own will be buried in a church yard. Not even my dog, Blue."

Pansy says the truth is that Dingo Duggernaut is too cheap to be a Christian. Too cheap to pay a $50 membership fee for the church plot. Too cheap to pay $15 per year for the graveyard committee's glorious beautification, restoration, and preservation plan, which Dingo says is a scheme to cheat them goody two-shoes churchgoers, and above all, too cheap to pay Mr. Minott to lay sister Peony out properly.

"God knows it costs money to be a Christian." Iris says that all the time.

On the day Pansy, Iris and Dingo went to the mortuary to make funeral arrangements, why, Dingo got out a dirty writing tablet from his overalls pocket, licked the end of his stubby pencil, and figured right fast that he didn't want to pay $850 for a casket, the cheapest one, $600 embalming fee, and a $50 hearse fee.

"Good gawd, a hearse fee?" Dingo yelled right in Mr. Minott's face.

"Yes," Mr. Minott crooned in a dignified voice, "To take the deceased from the mortuary to the church. Fifteen miles out there. And a $25 chapel fee."

"Good gawd, ride a dead woman in a limousine? A chapel fee?" yelled Dingo.

"Yes," Mr. Minott answered calmly. "$25 to rent the chapel here at the mortuary. There are more deceased than chapels, you know." Mr. Minott shook his list like a newspaper. "And $15 for Mrs. Burgandall to fix Peony's hair."

"Good gawd, like in a beauty parlor?" Spit flying crooked out of Dingo's mouth. "For a dead woman?"

Dingo Duggernaut swiped the list out of Mr. Minott's hand and read out loud. "Good gawd, the church needs $50 for the plot, a nice one in the shade?" Actually, this was Pansy's request but she kept quiet. Dingo shook his head over the list. "Peony needs shade? Good gawd, my cows need shade." Dingo ran his dirty fingernail under each item on the list. "Good gawd, the beautification committee needs $15 per year? Good gawd, a headstone? Good gawd, remember to give the minister a little something? Good gawd, make arrangements for music? Pay them a little something? What in the hell do you mean a spray for the top of Peony's coffin? Roses and carnations suggested?"

Dingo might have agreed to some things on Pansy and Iris's list except the argument about Peony's new dress came up. Dingo wanted to bury Peony in the best of her two cotton dresses. "What does a dead woman need with a new dress? Didn't need a new dress when she was alive, did she? Sure as hell don't need one now!"

Iris and Pansy pointed out to Dingo that both of Peony's dresses were patched. Patches on patches, if he would bother to look at them. "Dresses that look like scrap quilts," said Pansy, in that accusing way of hers. "We might as well wrap sister Peony in a quilt."

"Suits me," said Dingo.

Iris said she would offer one of her own dresses, but lord knows, you could put five Peonies in one of them.

Pansy said, yes, sister Peony was as thin as a gnawed bone because Dingo starved her, worked her like a pack animal. Peony came off big people. She never was thin before she married a Duggernaut. Always had apple cheeks and a sunny disposition. Look what marrying Dingo had done to her!

Dingo argued that if Iris and Pansy had ever worked a day in their lives they wouldn't be as wide as the broad side of the barn. Said their daddy spoiled them. Babied them. Said that's the reason no man would ever marry either one. Said they were both fat, ugly, and jealous that Peony had a man in her bed and they didn't!

"Peony had a boar hog in her bed," Iris blazed back. Reckoned that Dingo Duggernaut ought to look at himself in the mirror now and then. "Living with a hog killed sister Peony."

Well, Dingo wasn't paying $1,700 to bury a dead wife in a new dress. After all, Peony had left him high and dry with all the cows to milk, all the hay to put up, all the tobacco to grade and tie, all the cooking to do. All his dogs to feed. A cold bed. Said he hadn't got his mileage out of Peony.

Dingo vowed he wouldn't pay to bury Peony. He'd bury her at the back of the apple orchard. Or, by gawd, maybe he'd set her off at the county morgue on the way home and tell them to bury her at the poor farm graveyard. Said he didn't have time for digging a grave anyway.

"Wouldn't be legal," argued Mr. Minott, his back rigid as the spine of a book. "The law will see that you are responsible, Mr. Duggernaut. After all, she is your wife."

"Well, then?" said Dingo counting on his tobacco stained fingers, "What can I do legal that won't cost me for no casket, no embalming, no hearse, no hairdresser, no church, no chapel, no music, no minister, no beautification committee, no headstone, and no new dress?"

Mr. Minott said, after walking in circles and murmuring toward the funeral parlor ceiling and, finally, casting a sad glance toward sister Pansy and sister Iris, "We could cremate Peony."

"What would cremating cost?" asked Dingo, studying Mr. Minott with his good eye. Pansy stepped away from Dingo's walleye which she imagined cast across her with evil intent.

"About $250," said Mr. Minott, tapping his fingers together.

Next day, Peony Duggernaut was stripped naked and put in the oven. Iris and Pansy went into apoplexy seeing sister Peony stretched out thin and white like bread dough on a long bread pan, skin and bone naked in the presence of men. Dingo said only a fool would burn a perfectly good pine box. Peony didn't need one. Well, couldn't Mr. Minott put something over her, a sheet or a blanket, begged sister Iris. Dingo said he wasn't paying for no blanket either, so Mr. Minott rounded up an old silk casket lining, pink with lace around the edges.

Mr. Minott gave Pansy and Iris a cup of chamomile tea and convinced them to lie down in the chapel on a pew. He shook his head. Said there was nothing he could do to stop Dingo Duggernaut from having his wife cremated. Said cremating was a more dignified alternative than what Dingo had in mind. And wasn't it a god's shame Iris and Pansy must leave sister Peony alone with a heathen at the last event of her life?

When Peony was done, Mr. Minott brought out a blue urn with a lid, an urn like fine china with flowers and vines trailing around the base.

"Gawd no," says Dingo, "I won't pay $50 for no Grecian urn to store her ashes. I ain't got no mantel and wouldn't put Peony on it if I did."

Mr. Minott slashed the $50, plus tax, off Dingo's bill like cutting meat with a knife. "Guess you're going to haul Peony off in a slop bucket," says Mr. Minott, his shoulders thrown back, his mouth pressed together, his nostrils a flare, his chin quivery.

Dingo spied the Karo Syrup tin on a shelf in Mr. Minott's office. Pointed with his crooked finger. Said that tin would about fit Peony. Paid Mr. Minott two bucks for the tin. What it was worth, Dingo said.

Mr. Minott pulled Peony out of the oven, sifted her up in the dignified way a great chef would collect flour off a pastry board, and poured her into the Karo Syrup tin, still steaming. Dingo wasn't going to wait until she cooled. Said he had cows to feed and milk, had hay needed mowing, had tobacco to plant, had nitrate of soda to pick up at the Co-Op, had to stop up a leak in the barn roof, had to let his dogs out to run. They'd been penned up all day.

Iris and Pansy were mortified at the prospect of sister Peony in a syrup tin. They begged to buy the urn, said they'd pay the $50 out of the egg money. Dingo allowed he wouldn't use it even if they did. Well, then, could they have Peony's ashes? Dingo said, "No," spiteful thing that he is.

So, Dingo Duggernaut paid Mr. Minott $200, plus tax, for Peony's laying away. Said he was sorry he didn't think of it sooner, put Peony in the car, holding the hot tin between two work gloves, and sputtered toward home in his rusty old Rambler.

Pansy remarked with tears streaming down her face, "That's the first time Dingo Duggernaut has ever helped sister Peony into the car."

"Lord, woman," Iris cried into her handkerchief. "It may be the first time Peony's ever ridden in Dingo's car!"

It was Iris who hit upon the notion of using the Dustbuster to rescue sister Peony from the trunk of Dingo's Rambler where he put her after the cremation. On that day, Iris and Pansy went to the Co-Op to buy geraniums and impatiens. Dingo was backing his Rambler up to the loading dock, the trunk lid up so his blue tick hound, Blue, could ride. It was eagle-eyed Pansy who spotted the Karo Syrup tin in Dingo's open trunk. Blue, chasing fleas, was whacking the syrup tin with his big hind foot, making Peony gush out in white puffs like talcum powder.

Iris is adamant to this day that it was the voice of the Lord Jesus Christ Himself who instructed her to run across the street to Brown's Hardware and buy a Dustbuster that, miraculously, was on sale for $15.99. Mr. Brown took the Dustbuster out of the window and put in a fresh dirt bag and batteries. Iris paid him from a wad of bills she had hidden in her snuff can, then she hurried back across the street to the Co-Op. "Only God could have worked out this plan," Iris raised her face in praise toward heaven.

Pansy said the Lord had surely given her good eyesight for a reason. Said she would watch Dingo Duggernaut until he disappeared into the big dark mouth of the warehouse, until he was far enough back he couldn't see them against the light of noon outside, couldn't see them rescue Peony.

Pansy reported from the warehouse door. "Dingo's at the seed bin, dipping his hand into the Silver Queen corn. Now he's dipping in the bush beans, looks like." Iris, who couldn't see beyond the end of her nose, nodded. It was always Pansy who had to thread the needles, to fish out black specks from the cooking pot, to read the fine print on things.

"Dingo's shuffling off toward the fertilizers. He's stopping beside the lime. No. He's going back to the fertilizers. Looks like he's buying a hundred pound bag." Pansy hunkered beside the open door of the warehouse, held her hand as a visor above her eyes.

Dingo wound among the wooden pallets stacked high with sacks of red fescue, alfalfa, and red clover seed, stopping now and then to read the price tags, study the corn seed labels, or kick at a bag of soybeans. Pansy watched Dingo shrink farther and farther into the darkness of the warehouse.

"When Dingo gets to the Sevin Dust and the DDT, we must move quickly," said Pansy, holding her finger up like a track coach at the starting line. And when Dingo stopped before the tall rack of pesticides, Pansy shouted, "Go!"

The bottom of the Karo Syrup tin had rusted through. Bits of Peony were scattered among the wrenches and the pliers, sifted over the fishing tackle, worked to the edge of the floor mats, dusted over Blue's tail. From these places Pansy vacuumed a quart of dust and mud, working the nozzle in her plump hands around the trunk of the car as carefully as she vacuumed around the china cupboard, as gently as she vacuumed around the fern stands, as thoroughly as she cleaned the Indian rug before the fireplace. Pansy was bound to vacuum carefully. She couldn't tell how much was Peony, how much was dirt off Dingo's hunting boots, or how much of Peony had blown away.

Blue moved not an inch. Neither did he bark. Pansy held up Blue's tail between two fingers and sucked out another quart of dirt and mud. Then she vacuumed Blue's tail where she spied the telltale grey dust of sister Peony. Blue didn't flinch.

"The Lord has stilled Blue as he did the lion in the den," said Iris, prayer hands under her chin.

"Praise the Lord," said Pansy as she pried off the rusty lid of the syrup tin with a screwdriver from Dingo's toolbox, and sucked out the last dust of Peony. Iris emptied sister Peony's bone and gristle into a crumpled Food City grocery bag from Dingo's back seat. Pansy scattered dirt from the road around the trunk and scraped up rocks to refill the syrup tin. "The Lord's plan," she said.

"Dingo Duggernaut will find this out in hell," said Iris, shaking her round fist toward the dark inside of the warehouse.

On the way home, Iris and Pansy stopped at August Moon's Masonry, Ceramics, and Supply For Yard and Garden Home Center and bought the blue urn, eight gallon sized, with a huge Phoenix rising out of flames and ash, its wings spread for flight, its head proud toward the sky. Pansy was attracted to the urn straight away. She called it her American Eagle Urn. She bought two bags of fresh topsoil to mix with sister Peony's ashes. Iris suggested they plant peonies as a memorial. She bought the starter slips.

That spring, Pansy and Iris potted Peony in the large blue urn and set her on the porch steps, but just until the time came that she could be transplanted safely to the yard. Iris picked a spot beside the front gate. But now, if you drive by Pansy's and Iris's big old two storied white house on Mockingbird Lane, you'll see a large blue urn on the third stoop up, above the red geraniums, and below the impatiens. Growing out of the Phoenix and flames, you'll see huge double-red peonies burning in the sun.

Likely as not, Iris will be on the front porch, prowling among the woody trumpet vine winding up a white trellis, pinching the dead blooms, pressing her fingers in the dry soil around the geraniums, poking the spout of a watering can among the petunias. And from time to time, you will see Pansy standing on the steps, smiling over Peony.

After all their flowers have been tended, Iris and Pansy sit in their porch rockers. They look off toward the west when the sun is going down and chuckle as they study Dingo humped over his tractor and plow, inching his way like a dung beetle between the red clay field and the red horizon.

Black Dark

Mama makes me go through Mr. Fred's holler, and it black dark and me not able to see my hand in front of my eyes and night sounds coming at me ever which way. Owls screeching inside my head and feet swishing right by me in the leaves and me not seeing a thing, not knowing what it is. Mama doesn't know what it is like to run through bushes at night, brier vines clawing at my coat sleeves and possum vines trying to hang me by the neck like running into a clothes line in the dark, and stepping into holes I can't see.

But Mama says I must go through Mr. Fred's holler in black dark again if she needs to send me for help when the baby comes. I am almost nine now, she says, a big boy, not like two summers ago when Mama's pains came during the night hard and fast and Mama sent me to get Mr. Fred to come and drive her to the hospital. That's because Daddy is never home much. Daddy plays pinochle in the back of Shakey's pool room.

Mama says she's going to get dynamite someday and blow up Depot Street, one pool room after another. She's going to blow up all the beer joints and pool rooms where men go to hide from their families. She's going to blow them up one at a time and laugh while the whole street blazes to glory.

And what about Daddy? I say. *Are you going to blow him up too?*

And Mama says, *Yes.* She is going to blow up all of the dim rooms, the men who laugh with cigarettes shaking in the corners of their mouths, their eyes fixed on a deck of cards, their hands always readying for a mug. Mama shakes her head and says, *They plant not, neither do they reap.*

But mostly it is because of the money on the tables which can never be spent on ten pounds of potatoes, or a sack of sugar or coffee, or pretty things for the house, but because the money must always be spent on beer and more cards and laughing. Mama says playing the cards makes men hate their women and children and their homes, and the drinking makes men kill their unborn babies, like two years ago. So, she's going to blow it all up. And, also, I must go through the holler in black dark if need be, and I say, *Yes, Mama.*

Mama irons clothes beside the kitchen sink where the light comes in the little window. Her belly is big and moves itself against the edge of the ironing board. The light bulb in the kitchen is busted in the socket. There is no light and Daddy does not fix it.

And sometimes when Mama is ironing, Grandmama Caine comes knocking at the front door with a brown sack in her arms. Grandpa Caine brings Grandmama in his pickup and parks beside the great big bank in front of our house which sits on the road like Humpty Dumpty, and I can look down from the porch and see the rusted roof of his Ford. He sits and waits in the hot truck on Grandmama to get done with her visiting. Says he won't claim a daughter who runs off to marry a no-account, who breaks her parents' hearts. He has never been inside this house or in the other place we lived before. That was a little shingle house near the river.

I go out and sit in the truck with him sometimes while Mama and Grandmama talk. Grandpa Caine rubs my head with his big hand and says, *How's my boy?* Then he reaches way down in his overalls pocket and pulls up some change, fingering through a mess of washers and oats to find me a nickel. And I say, *Grandpa Caine, could I buy me a flashlight with this nickel at Birdsong's Store?* Grandpa laughs at me. I will not tell him I am afraid of the dark.

And Grandmama Caine comes in with her brown poke rattling cans of green beans, chow-chow and bread-and-butter pickles. She puts them on the table one by one out of the poke saying, *Here's a little something from me and your dad. And here's a can of pumpkin for pies.*

Grandmama Caine never looks at Mama. She sits and rubs her finger in a hole in the yellow checked table cloth. She asks Mama if she's put up much canning, and Mama says, *No, the garden isn't much this year.* Grandmama says she knows it's because Daddy doesn't help keep the garden up or plant a decent stand of beans and corn to begin with.

After while, Grandmama says she's heard a woman talking at the store. Mr. Fred may be getting shed of us. Daddy doesn't do his part on the farm anymore. Mr. Fred has put the word out for new renters. Mama runs the iron over the clothes the same as if she didn't hear.

Then, Mama whispers to the ironing board that Daddy was different before the war, before he learned bad things overseas in places not fit to live, in trenches, outside in the cold with the noise of bombs and bullets blasting inside his mind, in a place called the Bulge. *He's okay when he's not drinking. He's as good as any man when he's sober.* Grandmama says, *Huh! Your man comes off bad blood. He's no account like the rest of his people.* When we hear the red truck pull away from the bank, Mama cries up at the ceiling. *God, why have you forsaken me?*

I count Daddy home every night beside the open window with crickets and tree frogs screaming in the dark. They scream without stopping until morning because they are afraid. As long as they can answer themselves, they know they are alive in the dark.

I hear myself count to sixty over and over until he comes. Daddy's junk car rolls in slow beside the bank, and he parks in the worn, muddy ruts. His car door shuts loud and the tree frogs stop screaming for a second of silence. Then, his big boots stomp up the plank steps against the bank. His boots stomp along the short walk Mama made from a sack of concrete Mr. Fred gave her to keep the mud from tracking in. Daddy stops and pees in the pretty-by-nights Mama planted along the front porch. She is proud of her flowers, and in the evening she waters them, and holds their little chins in her fingers and smiles.

Sometimes Daddy gets us out of bed in the night. He wants the lights on. He wants food on the table. *Where is the meat,* he says. *A man needs meat. It is almost morning,* Mama says back. *Go to sleep. You'll wake the boy.* She sees me peeping out of my room in the dark. The baby churns under Mama's gown. *Damn you*, he says. I see his hand go back and hear it crack like a whip against Mama's face. She screams, *Get behind the door! Behind the door*!

I have a hidey-hole in the corner behind my big oak door. I have wooden spools for soldiers and tin cans for my fort. And there is a big crack where the hinges are when the door is opened back into the corner, and that is my spy hole. I have a rope that Grandpa gave me out of his truck. Inside my hidey-hole, I tie the rope around the doorknob that is white and smooth as a hen's egg. Then I tie it around a big nail, as big as Daddy's fingers, hammered in the floor. But this is for the day.

For night, I put the rope around the nail and then around my hands and hold tight. Behind the door, I listen to Daddy's boots walking crooked across the floor boards. The living room light comes to the crack along the hinges and I can hear Mama screaming, *Get behind the door!* And I can hear my body screaming inside like tree frogs. Inside my body comes Mama's screaming, and then she does not scream anymore. Through my spy hole, I see the soles of Mama's feet.

Daddy's boots stomp toward the door, then in the crack comes his big eye, nervous like a horse's. He tries to see into the dark, but his big body blocks the light. Something burns inside my head, and the rope burns my hands. After while, his boots stomp away, but they come back fast. His eye is back again, and then comes his breath through the crack like rotten potatoes. He pulls hard on the loose doorknob, and it rattles like bolts in a can. The rope jerks through my fingers burning hot. He says, *Come out of there boy!* The side of his sweaty face is flashing in the living room light. I pull the rope tighter. *Thank you God. Thank you for the dark behind this door.*

I love you Mama. I love you. When I grow up I'm going to buy you that candy dress, red and white striped in Powell and Sandel's, the one you stop and gaze at through the window and lick your lips for. The sandals, too. White patent leather you called them. I will have money then, lots of money, and we will shop on Saturday morning. After the dress, we will go the Corner Drug, and I will order two chocolate sodas the way we like them in tall glasses with straws. We will sit on the stools and swivel round and round, even if the drugstore man shakes his finger and says, *No.*

Mr. Fred says we must not mess up his car. It is a new '57 Plymouth with grey inside like touching velvet cloth. I promise him the baby will not mess up his car, if only he will please hurry.

His shirt hangs out of his pants. His eyes come in angry slits like a dog about to growl when he sees Daddy snoring across the bed, and Mama lying in a round, wet spot on the wooden floor. Mr. Fred puts me in the front and Mama lies on the back seat. We start up the road, and Mama screams, *The baby is coming. Now,* she says, *Now!* Mr.

Fred pulls into his own driveway. He blows his car horn, and then Misses Fred is standing under the yellow bulb on the back porch. Misses Fred goes inside the house, and then she comes to the car through the yellow light with something in her hand. Towels.

Mama cries in the back seat. I cannot see her face. Mr. Fred tells me to go behind the car and stand. Misses Fred gets into the back of the car and after awhile she gets out again. She takes the soft bundle of towels toward the yellow light in front of her like a plate of hot biscuits. There is no sound of screaming in the dark, not even the tree frogs. Mr. Fred's car is shiny slick behind, and when I put my fingers on it, I can feel Mama crying in the bumper.

I love you Mama. When I grow up, we will have a house much bigger than this one of Mr. Fred's. It will be bright white like blazing sun with big round poles to hold up the porch. We will live along the river and have rocking chairs on the porch like in magazines, and we will rock in the chairs where breezes will come to fan our faces in the afternoon. We will have a rug on our floor, and plenty of pretty curtains for our house. We will have a better car than Mr. Fred's with velvet seats, and a good flashlight so I will not be afraid to walk through the holler in the dark.

Mr. Fred's holler is shaped like Daddy's car, and when we drive through it, the morning sun on the windshield looks like a spider's web. Mama says that it is dangerous. She says the whole glass could bust out in our faces before we could say jack-in-the-box. Daddy says, *Shut up*, around the cigarette in his mouth. Mama gets quiet, mostly because her belly hurts and she is bent over in the front seat. She jerks the handle so hard the door flies open on Mr. Fred's curve, and Daddy grabs her in. *For God's sake, lock that door,* he says. Daddy goes too fast, she says back. And then Mama starts the crying again.

Daddy says we must have the funeral ourselves. There is no money for a blue casket with a white lining like Mama wanted. No money for the fancy undertakers. They smile at you like they are friends, but they only want money, he says. Two years ago them undertakers took half the tobacco crop. *Yes*, Mama whispers back, *and still no rock to mark his grave, to mark his coming and going*.

When we get to Birdsong's store, two men are standing on the porch. One is Mr. Akers of the Dixon Mill who grinds Mama's corn. A great noisy machine makes the cornmeal. The cobs go in a metal mouth on one side, and yellow meal flies out the spout on the other side. I like to feel it snowing though my fingers into the sack. Another man I do not know is drinking a dope with his hand on his hip. They stare at us like we are pictures in a book and do not speak.

Daddy pumps the gas and goes inside to pay. He walks around them like trees. He comes out with wooden crates under his arms and dangling off his hands. He puts the crates in the trunk, and ties the lid with twine to keep them in. Through the window, he hands Mama a B.C. Powder and a chocolate dope, the kind she likes. *Didn't you get the boy one, s*he says. Mama hands me her chocolate dope across the seat. It tastes grainy and bitter like Epsom Salts around the rim.

Across the road, the children are in the school behind the big windows that go from top to bottom and have many squares. *When we settle in at Mr. Fred's, I will send the boy to Walker's School,* I heard Mama say to Daddy when we moved into Mr. Fred's house. At Walker's School I will learn to make A's like Indian tee-pees, and S's like snakes, and T's like crosses, and D's like a waxing moon, and C's like a moon in wane. Mama tells me that is how I will know my letters, and then I will make them words. Mama shows me how to draw the snakes and crosses and the moons with a pencil on a grocery bag.

Daddy says there is no need for learning words. No need to send the boy to Walker's School, or any school. *Woman, you want to shame me by sending the boy to school. Look. I lived through a war, dammit. I thought I was dead a thousand times. Don't you make light of me!*

But the boy is almost nine, she says back. *You know how to read a deck of cards, let the boy learn to read books.*

And now I will not go to Walker's School. We must leave the house that sits like Humpty Dumpty on our bank, and I wave out the car to the children who read behind the windows.

The children do not know me, or that I can count to sixty. Mama says I must not tell Daddy that I can draw the numbers along the edge of the magazine with pretty houses, or say them in my mind.

When we are driving on the road I try to count the trees that pass by the car windows. They go too fast. But I can count the seven houses on the windey-road by Granny Lewis Creek, and the two at Tilson's Gap, houses with flowers by the porch. One house has a clothesline with overalls and blue jeans walking on the wind. I count a big man and six strapping boys living on this clothesline.

After the mountain there are no more houses to count, and so I watch the road run by the rusty hole in the floor board, blurry, like going round and round. I can not stop looking at it. *The boy is sick,* Mama says. *He's had nothing but a bite of pone and milk since morning.* Daddy says we will be at Aunt Spivey's by supper. There is only money for gas.

Aunt Spivey is on the front steps wiping her hands on the bottom of her apron when we drive up her crooked road. Her face is figuring out our car.

We can go back and get the stuff later, Daddy tells Mama. When I can borrow a truck. Aunt Spivey will let us put it in her barn until we get a place.

The bundle is wrapped around and around with towels, tight, like a big white egg. Mama says, *Hand the baby up. I will carry it myself.* It smells like a ripe mushmellon. I shake my head, no. Daddy says he will come around and get it for her.

Aunt Spivey comes to the car wringing her hands on the bottom of her apron. She leans half-way into the car. *Laws me. What is this?* she says. Her gums are pinkey-red when she opens her mouth to look at our dead baby wrapped up like an egg in Misses Fred's towels.

There is a feast of food on Aunt Spivey's table. Streaky meat and beans, sliced tomatoes, fried potatoes with onions. And lots of buttermilk. There is a blackberry cobbler with warm milk for afters. Aunt Spivey says, *Laws, I'd have cooked more if I'd a knowed you was coming.*

Mama does not eat. She sits beside the window watching up the hill where Daddy hammers the boards together from the wooden crates out of the trunk. Aunt Spivey says it is best for Mama to rest. She puts Mama's feet into a pan of steamy water to ward off cold. Aunt Spivey says she will bind Mama's belly tight with strips of white cloth she tears from a sheet to make her go back right. Aunt

Spivey rubs lard on the side of Mama's face that is purple, and rubs around her eye that is swelled shut. Her brown fingers are like knobby twigs of kindling. *Laws have mercy, why put up with a man like that?* She shakes her fist at the window where Daddy is framed like a picture on the hill with the wooden box and his shovel digging. *If he wasn't my kin, I'd of lawed him myself*, she says.

Mama says to Aunt Spivey that Daddy can not help himself. Her voice is the same as when the two men from the Birdsong's Store came and found Daddy on the bed asleep, and Mr. Akers jerked him up while the one I do not know punched into his belly. And Mama said, *Stop. Stop. He can not help it. He doesn't mean to do it. Leave us alone*. Daddy was asleep and could not feel their fists, so the two men dropped him on the floor like a rag. They looked hard at Mama with questions in their eyes, and went away.

There has been a storm, but only the trees are raining now. Mama starts the crying again. *Won't the water get to my lamb*? she says. Aunt Spivey rubs a white cloth with lard to wrap the baby in and Mama hushes.

I love you Mama. When I grown up and have lots of money, I will buy you a blue box with a white lining for our baby, the way you like it. And I will also buy a rock for our other baby to mark its coming and going. And I will go to Walker's School and make words of the crosses and moons. We will sit on the porch swing of a late afternoon and read my words with your fingers under them, and swing and swing.

Daddy cannot sleep here. Aunt Spivey held him out with her broom handle across the door like a gun. He would not cross her path. Aunt Spivey says that she is ashamed to claim Daddy as kin, and that is why he is gone. I have never seen Daddy afraid of anyone before, but he did not cross the old woman with her broom-gun across the door. Daddy shouts inside to Mama that he will come back and fetch her when he has found a place. Aunt Spivey tells him he will find his place in hell. He goes away and we hear his car drive over the rocks into the dark.

Mama will sleep in Aunt Spivey's big bed. Mama lies atop the bed as cold and still as a chunk of stove wood. I can see her eyes jump back and forth under the clearness of her lids. One side of

Mama's face is white like a plate, and the other side is like the rotten belly of a cucumber. Aunt Spivey tucks a pieced quilt of many scraps around Mama.

Aunt Spivey says Mama is sick because she has bled too much. That is why she is limp as a dishrag. Aunt Spivey says she can cure the fever and stop the blood. It is a gift she has. She will use cold rags and willow bark tea and many prayers.

Mama is beautiful and still like the marble lady who lies atop her grave at the New Ebenezer Presbyterian Church. Mama says the marble lady belonged to a rich family who can afford such trifles. Amanda Winfield Evans, the grave says.

When Daddy is not home and we must walk to Birdsong's Store, Mama takes me across the road and up the hills, and we walk among the dead people and read their graves. Mama puts her fingers on the words and says them out loud, *Here Lies Amanda Winfield Evans, Beloved Wife of Jacob Evans*. I do not like to see the cold, marble lady asleep atop her own grave, but I like to read the words.

It is really our dead baby buried near the fence row along the graveyard that Mama comes to see. He is marked with a pile of rocks and a peach sapling that Mama planted on his head.

And now Mama is like the marble lady, quiet and still, and Aunt Spivey sits beside her with the cold rags and her tonic in a snuff glass. Aunt Spivey is very old. She wears dresses old-woman long that slosh about her ankles. Her skin is yellow like old wallpaper and her voice does not sing the words like Mama does. She is reading her cures from the Book of Ezekiel. When she sucks in and out with her mouth open, her breath smells like turpentine. But she has twinkly eyes, and she is good to help Mama who is not even her blood kin. It is Daddy who belongs to her family, her great-nephew on her brother's side.

Aunt Spivey will sleep sitting in her chair beside Mama's bed, and I will sleep on a pallet of quilts Aunt Spivey made for me on the living room floor. My pallet smells like Aunt Spivey's cedar chest. She sets out a clean paint bucket if I need to make water in the night. I have a good ham biscuit I saved in my pocket to eat under the covers.

A kerosene lamp beside Mama's bed licks its flame against the dark window. It licks and licks at the black night, and only the lamp to hold back all that darkness. I want to tell my Mama and Aunt Spivey to guard the lamp. They will only say, *Hush now. Go to sleep. It will be morning soon.* Outside the tree frogs are silent, and I am afraid before morning comes the dark will push in through the window.

Doomsday Monday at Pee Wee's Hamburger Emporium

See. It happened like this. It's a Monday. Lunch time. I'm on French fries. Herman's on the buns. Cherry's running the drive-through. Our dip-stick manager, Sammy Dedmon, is making burgers, patting them out real sloppy in his fat dimpled hands. I'm dipping the crinkles into the hot grease, two baskets full and two more ready when these come out. It's a boom day for a Monday. Nothing like you'd expect. People lined up in five rows at the counter, and a line of cars backed up from the drive-through window all the way out to the Wiley Dixon Highway. Some convention at the big Baptist church downtown. Five, maybe six hundred Baptists coming in from Bangkok to Kalamazoo, and our hamburger joint the only one in ten miles, either side of us, and only four of us on duty, dancing to keep up with the orders.

Normally, we can feed half the town of Dixon without a hitch. But our short order chef, Johnny Frizzell, is laying out of work again, so Sammy, the new manager, is grilling. As if he's got the talent to slap hamburgers like Johnny Frizzell. Johnny's a master short order grill man. Been at it all his life. He could slap out 500 burgers in a blitz. But this new manager we just got, Sammy Dedmon, he's too much a dufus to call in the back-up cook, Norma Gentry, who can slap and fry burgers nearly as good as Johnny.

No, Sammy ain't done a sensible thing in the two weeks he's been working here at Pee Wee's Hamburger Emporium, serving the best burgers and fries money can buy. You can see our sign towering 50 feet over the Emporium just off highway 181 going south toward Asheville. We live up to our name, because that's the kind of class we have. Me, Gilbert Grubbs, Junior, I've been here three years next month, and I'm the best damn fry-baby this side of Morgan City.

I says to Sammy, "Why don't you call in Norma Gentry. She won't mind coming in on short notice." I say this because Norma always comes in when Johnny is laying out. It's understood.

Sammy looks over at me with his pole-axed expression, and then he shoots me this textbook bull about the responsibility of a manager to be sensitive to his employees. Sammy says Norma works too hard, and too many long hours, always having to fill in for Johnny while he's off drunk.

"Norma's not a young woman any more," Sammy says. "She's worked the night shift and cleaned up. Besides, her son and his family have come to visit, and the decent thing to do is leave Norma in peace and do the best we can."

No. Norma ain't young anymore, but she's the kind that's like your mama. If you whine, she'll do just about anything you want her to, even if she's worked her fingers to the bone. She's that responsible kind that feels guilty, and if you know how to suck up the right way you can get her to stay late and clean up the meat grinder, even when it's your turn and she's already stayed late three nights in a row.

Working weekends at the Emporium, now that's what messes up your social life. We don't close until 11 p.m. on weekdays, and 12 midnight on weekends. In a town like Dixon where everybody's parents go to bed with the roosters, and all the sweet young things got to get their prissy selves in by 11 o'clock, well, you can see how it is. So, me and Johnny know how to play up to Norma, how to plead and give her that sweet peck on the cheek and tell her how pretty she's looking these days, even if she's sixty something and has more chins than an pug dog, and good old Norma will stay and mop the kitchen, and clean the tables. Yeah, Norma is the dependable type, every time. She's been working at the Emporium since she was forty. Her old man just up and left her about ten years ago, so what else has she got to worry about anyway?

Well, I got to defend Johnny because he's my buddy. My hero. So I says to Sammy, "You've got to respect a real talent like Johnny Frizzell. Johnny makes the best burgers in Dixon, or Monroe City for that matter. He knows how to mix fresh ground chuck with sirloin, just the right amounts, how to put in secret seasonings, and how to shape the meat just right so them burgers come up juicy and lean. He's a real artist."

Besides, there's nothing exciting to do in a one-light town like Dixon, but get drunk or get some loving. Better if it's both together. Johnny's got this real talent with women, too, and every once in a while he's got to have a big weekend. Usually, Johnny lays out on a Monday. I says to Sammy that it ain't Johnny's fault. Monday's most always a dud day.

Sammy takes off his round spectacles with the wire rims and while he's blowing fog on the lenses and rubbing them on his shirtsleeve, he gives me a sermon about Johnny Frizzell. How talent ain't nothing without responsibility. He looks at me over the rims of his glasses where he's set them down on the edge of his nose. When Sammy starts talking about respect, all I can think of is Mr. Whipple in the toilet paper commercial saying, "Please don't squeeze the Charmin! Please don't squeeze the Charmin!" and how Sammy Dedmon looks like Mr. Whipple and what a stupid word respect is when Sammy Dedmon is preaching it. I'm thinking Sammy Dedmon ain't been loved by a woman in his life.

When Johnny's laying out, we've all learned how to roll with the punches. That is, Norma Gentry, she grills on the afternoon and evening shift, and anytime else she's needed, and Herman Little, who builds the burgers and lays them on the plate, and Cherry Berry, who works the drive-through window and the cash register. And yours truly, Gilbert Grubbs. I make the fries, pour the drinks, and make the shakes. All of us are supposed to take turns on clean-up duty.

Doomsday Monday ain't all Johnny's fault, though. He didn't know anymore than we did about the Baptist convention. And Johnny had to do something about Cherry Berry. See, Johnny used to have the hots for Cherry. She's only 17 and about as dumb as a coal bucket, which is why Johnny, who is 38 if he's a day, kind of got fed up with baby-sitting. He told me one day how getting the taco was great, but listening to all that whiny bull about her parents and how they was too strict and how Cherry was going to run away from home and could she move in with Johnny made him feel like he'd just had a cold shower.

Cherry Berry is a dumb little trick, but it doesn't take a genius to figure out that Johnny Frizzell is trying to cut it off with her. Johnny's way to end a fling is to go cold turkey. Get him a hot date and make sure the girl he's trying to ditch finds out about it, which ain't hard in a town with a population of 538. But I sure as hell ain't going to tell Sammy that Johnny has been getting it with Cherry and now he wants to cut her off. That's why he's laying out.

Cherry comes in today moaning, "Where's Johnny? You seen him?" She's all flushed-faced and there's a row of salty sweat beads on her upper lip that I'd like to lick off. I'm looking at curves finer than a Barbie Doll's and not really concentrating on what Cherry is saying.

Herman winks at me and says to Cherry, "He's had a hot weekend. Probably got him some sweet young thing."

You can see Cherry is about to bust out in tears when she goes running off toward the girls' bathroom, her chest all swelled up from hitching her breath and holding it the way girls do when they get upset.

Herman is the kind of guy that likes to rub salt in a wound. He's scrawny with long arms that hang way out of his shirtsleeves. His face looks like a pepperoni pizza most of the time. He's just pissed that Cherry don't pay him no mind. Me, I wouldn't have gone that far saying the things he said to Cherry. I'm the quiet kind of guy that likes to be around to pick up the pieces. I'm not pretty-boy handsome like Johnny, who kind of looks like the Fonz, leather jacket and motorcycle, too. But I sure as hell know how to be sensitive to a girl just busted up in love. Johnny taught me a trick or two, and when I feel the time is right, I'll make my move. After all, Cherry is a hot piece with a pointy little nose and a nice round bottom that looks like a valentine walking on long legs.

So here we are on a Monday when the staff is usually cut back, and there's five hundred hungry Baptists lined up for burgers and fries, and Sammy's back here at the grill, mostly standing in the way acting like he knows what he's doing. He don't know diddly-squat.

Sammy's still wearing his nice white shirt and his navy blue power suit. He's got his shirt unbuttoned, though, and his yellow paisley tie hanging loose around his neck. Sammy doesn't even put on an apron. He's got grease spattered up and down the front of his shirt already. It must be 110 degrees back here. The air conditioning ain't worked right in a year, and Sammy's hunching over the dizzy heat of that big flat grill, sweating like a pig, waving the steam off with the long, metal spatula, flipping rows and rows of hamburgers like they was pancakes, burning some of them around the edges. He can't even see them hamburgers through the greasy steam, and ain't got sense enough to turn the grill down. Me and Herman wink at each other over a long row of Styrofoam plates with open buns on them, and don't say a thing. Let him burn the whole bunch of burgers. Serves him right.

Sammy's face is puffed up red and greasy. He's breathing hard and wiping his face with a dishtowel. Me and Herman see that he can't take the heat like we can. Sammy's roasted to about medium rare. That's when all hell breaks loose. A little old Grandma Moses standing back in that sardine crowd of church goers starts shouting, "Where's the beef? Where's the beef?" Everybody turns around and looks.

"We've got to speed things up," I say to Sammy. "Fries are getting cold already." Sammy looks back over his shoulder at that whole congregation of hungry Baptist faces looking like they've been weaned on sour milk. I can see Sammy's mind jump out of his skull. Sammy gets so nervous he grabs another greasy spatula and unloads the whole grill with both hands flipping burgers everywhere, me and Herman trying to catch them before they slide off the plates. Two big ones go over the edge of the grill and land, kerplunk, right on Sammy's feet.

About the same time that the little lady in her Sunday hat and gloves is playing like she's in a TV commercial, the cars lined up outside the drive-through window start honking. I see out the window the cars backed all the way out the Emporium's circular drive and into the main street of Dixon, backed down farther than I can see. And I got four baskets of fries out of the grease and getting cold. Now, we got us a real crisis.

I've never seen this many Baptists in one place in all my life. Seems like a hundred wrinkled Sunday faces bobbing like the Saint Vitus Dance, some high and some low, and a hushy murmur of voices like the wind humming. And they've got this peculiar smell about them like mothballs, rosewater, Ben Gay, and Old Spice, all mixed and mingled together with the smell of hamburgers and French fries.

Cherry is working the drive-through window and the counter, too, racing from one side of the Emporium to the other, racing from the cash register to the counter to the window to the cash register. There's only one cash register so she's got to run across from the window to the other side of the counter and ring up the sales. Cherry keeps dropping money on the floor because the Emporium cash register is an old antique model made back in the 1930's and the drawers ain't deep enough. The register makes a peculiar sound like crunch-crunch-tinkle-tinkle-ding every time Cherry rings up a sale, which is about every 30 seconds. Every few minutes Cherry scrapes the bills out of the overflowing drawer and runs off to the back of the Emporium.

Cherry's face is wet and swollen from crying over Johnny Frizzell, and her baby blond curls are coming loose from under her golden Emporium hat. She's ringing up sales, stuffing them Baptist bills in the register, and wiping her eyes on her uniform sleeves. Cherry has this kind of frozen dumb look on her face that says, "Help me! Help me!" I look over at sweet Cherry with tears running down her face, a ten-dollar bill clenched between her teeth, her hands making swift change from the cash register, and I could almost cry.

Herman is crying, too. He's got onions shooting out of the slicer like it's a Frisbee machine, and a whole pile of tomatoes lined up on the counter. Hell, he hasn't even had time to rinse the grit off the lettuce leaves, but what's a man to do when the mob is beating down the jailhouse door? I see Sammy running toward the back and saying, "Thank you God," when he finds five more bags of hamburger buns, 50 count each. Lucky thing the Rainbow bread man just made a delivery this morning. We ran out of ketchup, though. What a bummer.

Sammy still has the grill turned up too high, and a big cloud of grease and smoke rolls out across the counter and chokes the customers pushed up at the front, sends them into a coughing frenzy, waving their arms and their pocketbooks. Hell, it looks like the gas chamber at the state pen. That's when Sammy finally asks me how to turn the heat down. I go over to the grill and point to the controls along the right side. What a dumb head. Sammy refunds at least fifteen people who say their burgers taste like old ground up newspapers. They're real nice about it, considering they had to stand there for an hour and wait on their burgers in the first place. Sammy is hangdog sorry, and gives them a free milk shake. We ran out of meat, so he can't fry them another burger.

Well, what do you expect when you get a new manager that ain't never worked the ropes. Sammy got him one of them degrees in restaurant management from the Dixon Community College. But he ain't never worked short order, or wiped tables, or rung up sales, or mopped floors. Nothing. Sammy ain't never run a meat grinder or cleaned it up. It's a monster grinder that takes fifty pounds of meat at a time. He heaves them big trays of fresh meat out of the cooler, balances them above the top of his head, and dumps in whole sirloin roasts without trimming them or cutting them up in chunks. He forgets to add the chuck, forgets to layer the meat in the grinder with the seasonings. If you run a grinder right it makes a soft purring sound and that meat oozes out real lean and fine. When Sammy runs the grinder, it groans and coughs.

Sammy can't be taught a thing. Sammy's one of them book worms. Thinks books got all the answers. How did he learn about managing hamburger emporiums, I ask you? Going around to restaurants all over East Tennessee, taking notes on a clipboard and observing. Observing? What kind of nonsense is that? Sammy calls it fieldwork. Now don't that beat all. My old man, Gilbert Grubbs, Senior, he can tell you all about field work. He can tell you about plowing fields and planting acres of wheat and corn, about mowing and picking and spudding tobacco. That's what my old man calls field work. That's why I stay away from fieldwork.

Sammy is always holding forth on human relations skills, money skills, and management skills and claims that if you get you a restaurant management degree you don't have to start on the bottom doing drudgework. You can get you one of them entry-level positions and wear a suit and a tie. Sammy says I ought to think serious about becoming a restaurant manager. "Gilbert," he says one day when I'm cleaning out the grinder with disinfectant, my hands full of red hamburger worms I'm pushing out of the feeder snout, and he's sitting on his behind looking at me like he knows something, "You need to get your GED and get into the community college like I did. Worry about your future, Gilbert. I mean it."

I says to myself, "Sammy, you don't know your elbow from third base. Spending good money and wasting time with your nose in a book, and here you are manager, can't do a sensible thing, and making $5 less per hour than Johnny Frizzell, who's the best damn hamburger man in the business. A man with real talent." I try to picture Johnny with a book and a clipboard. Nah.

That's what the inside of my head is saying to Sammy, but I say,

"Sure, Sammy. I'll think about it." I figure I'll tell him what he wants to hear. I'll be here at the Emporium long after dipstick Sammy gets his soft round rear-end booted out. Which won't be long when old Pee Wee Duncan, who founded the Emporium back in 1959 and made it what it is today, comes in here and sees how the dufus does things.

Pee Wee's gone off for a month on business down to Florida. At least, that's what he told the old lady Duncan. Supposed to be buying restaurant equipment since he's going to open up a new branch of the Emporium in Morgan City, thirteen miles up the road. But Johnny tells me the other day that Pee Wee is mixing his business with pleasure, if you know what I mean.

Pee Wee hadn't been gone a week when our old manager, Booger Red Luttrell, died right there on top of the hamburger grill one night after we closed. Booger Red must have been cleaning it, because Johnny found him next morning bent belly down across the grill with his feet still on the floor and his arms reaching out toward the meat grinder. Coroner said it was a heart attack, and if the grill had been on, why Booger Red would have been done to a cinder and we'd never know the cause of death. Booger Red managed the Emporium for 30 years. He was a real pro, I want to tell you.

Anyway, when old lady Duncan saw Booger-Red gone rigor mortis on the grill, and she couldn't get in touch with Pee Wee down in Florida because no one answered the number he left, well, she went crazy wild.

Now, I don't believe in fortune and fate, mind you, but wouldn't you know it, Sammy Dedmon, just graduated from the Dixon Community College with his degree in restaurant management, comes along in his blue polyester suit, his white shirt, and yellow paisley tie carrying a whole stack of resumes he's been passing out at restaurants all up and down Highway 181.

Old lady Duncan takes one look at fat little Sammy in his power suit and his white shirt and thinks he's the answer to her prayers. She says, "Sammy, you're hired," and then she calls her cousin Benny to go off to Florida and find Pee Wee. Johnny Frizzell tells me in strictest confidence that he knows where Pee Wee is stashed at a Florida resort with Germaine Deal, the cute redheaded girl who works at Motlow's Florist and Gift Shop on Main Street. He ain't saying a thing, though.

Why stick your nose in something that ain't none of your business.

Somehow, we pull off a restaurant miracle. Sammy is lucky this ain't a bankers' convention or a mob of hungry insurance salesmen. Might as well have your tail caught in the lawn mower. But these Baptists, they're genteel types. You can see they're pissed, though, by the way their faces go solemn, their lips get set in this straight, stiff line and a deep crinkle comes up over their eyes. A whole crowd of them with their arms crossed, but not saying a thing, just letting out a sigh once in a while like a ketchup bottle opened after it's been standing in the heat. It's that damned patient silence that drives you crazy.

By three in the afternoon we got the five thousand fed, and they ain't but two couples sitting in the Emporium. One couple I know, Pete and Dora Sauceman, came in after the big crowd for milk shakes. The other couple must be with the Baptist group. He's a skinny feller with a dark suit on, and dad-burned if the blond don't weigh 350 pounds and she's wedged between the little plastic swivel seat and the little plastic table like a crooked quarter in a slot machine. She's got this peculiar look on her face like she's got gas on her stomach. Her nervous husband keeps coming over to the counter asking for another co-cola, but he's the one drinking them.

Finally, Pete and Dora suck dry and leave, and the only customers left is Jack Sprat and his fat wife sitting by the window squished up in the red plastic swivel seat with her belly all limbered out like syrup and oozing over the top of the yellow plastic table.

Sammy is trying to clean the grill, Herman is taking out the trash and then he's going to the butcher shop for more meat, and Cherry is throwing her apron on the floor, and running back to the girls' bathroom crying. I want to say something comforting to Cherry, like, "I know how you're feeling, Cherry. I'm here if you need me, Cherry," that kind of bull that a girl always falls for.

I'm standing over the grease vats shaking out two fryer baskets in each hand, wondering if this grease will make it another day or two and thinking that maybe it's not the time to make my move on Cherry, and what would Johnny Frizzell do in a situation like this, when the nervous little feller comes up to the counter and says, "My wife and I are in a rather peculiar situation over here, and I wonder if you might help us?" He's got this daintified voice, a soft mannered guy with prissy hands and clean fingernails. He looks at you over the tops of his glasses with that concerned face that religious people get.

I put down the baskets and take off my apron. The nervous little feller runs ahead of me, then looks back and says in a whisper, "Come here. Come here," with his pointer finger wiggling me over. Well, as if I can't see as far as the windows. The Emporium ain't but 20 feet deep and 25 feet wide. Anyway, the man introduces himself real polite, "I'm Rupert Dearstone and this is my wife, Tizzie. And it seems as if we've got ourselves into something of a predicament."

And before Rupert Dearstone can tell me what's the matter, this Tizzie starts bawling. To get right to the point, Tizzie is stuck in Pee Wee's new plastic seat and table that he bought at an equipment auction over in Charlotte, North Carolina, last month. We just had all the old booths taken out and twenty of these fancy two-seater tables with plastic swivel chairs put in. Pee Wee figured we could seat forty people instead of the twenty we could handle before. Pee Wee says this is the rocket age, and progress is always necessary if you want to get ahead. And besides, expanding with new tables is cheaper than building on.

The way Rupert tells it, Tizzie gets herself swiveled into the seat when they first get here, and he stands in line for the order while she holds their seats, but then after Tizzie eats four half-pounder Emporiums, lettuce, tomato, onion, mayo, and four large orders of crinkles, no ketchup, and two vanilla milk shakes and two co-colas, she can't swivel out. And here's Tizzie bloated up between the chair and the table, the table's edge looking like it's slicing her in two.

First, I tell Rupert to get behind Tizzie and pull back on the seat, and I'll get hold of the table on the other side and pull the opposite direction. Tizzie is supposed to wiggle out the side when we loosen the seat. Rupert gives Tizzie's seat a heave-ho, turns red-faced like he's going to blow his guts out his nose, and I pull on the table with my heels dug into the plastic molding. Nothing happens. Pee Wee's plastic tables and chairs come in one piece. They're bolted to the walls and the floors. Space-age plastic don't budge.

Tizzie is really panicking. In that lime green dress, she looks like a giant Jell-O trying to fly. Her gigantic arms flap above her gigantic belly which has pushed up to the top of her chest where her heart would normally be, and her chest has pushed her titties under her chin.

She says she'll suffocate and die if we don't get her out this minute. Says she's been stuck over two hours, and our salty, green-tasting hamburgers are making her swell up. Besides which she's sick to her stomach and thinks she's been poisoned.

Tizzie's face is puffy and pink like a Miss Piggy balloon, and it starts to float and bob around and around until she flat out faints and goes limp all over the table, dissolving into a big puddle of blubber. You'd swear that Pee Wee's new swivel table and chair had disappeared before your eyes.

Rupert goes into hysterics and starts crying, "Please help her, please help her!" He's sobbing and shaking his hands and running in circles. Sammy comes around the counter to see what's causing the commotion.

"Oh, my goodness, Gilbert. Get some wet paper towels and put on her face," he screams at me. Then he runs out the door and around the building. I don't know where in the hell Sammy's gone, but in a minute he comes back in with a crow bar. Sammy dances around and waves the crow bar, trying to find a place to wedge it so he can pry the table loose from the wall. There ain't no place to wedge the crow bar that Tizzie Dearstone ain't melted all over. She's still out of it and breathing in loud guffs.

Well, while Sammy Dedmon and Rupert Dearstone are running in circles, me, Gilbert Grubbs, Junior, takes the simple approach. I dial 9-1-1 and tell Monroe Lamb at the rescue squad to get his butt off that chair he sits propped in every day and bring a saw. We got a woman dying up here at the Emporium. Any damn fool can see by now the only way to get Tizzie Dearstone out of that plastic chair is to saw her out.

Monroe Lamb never does anything unless he does it big. He gets to the Emporium quick as a wink because he's only two blocks down the street, and he brings the rescue truck, the fire department, and five patrol cruisers, and they're sitting out in front of the Emporium with the blue lights and sirens blasting away. You never heard such a racket since the Lowman's Arsenal on Pigeon Creek blew up a few years ago. The newspaper said that a woman named Teresa Green forgot the company rules, DANGER, DANGER. VOLATILE MATERIALS. NO NYLON HOSE ALLOWED BEYOND THIS POINT. Teresa generated static electricity between her legs that blew up a vat of ether. People from over in Morgan City said it knocked the glasses out of their cabinets. What can I say? We don't have many emergencies here in Dixon, but when we do, we go all out.

Monroe Lamb saunters into the Emporium, nonchalant, with a chain saw dangling on his leg like he's Clint Eastwood in a spaghetti western. Half a dozen firemen and four sheriff's deputies come in behind. "What's the situation here?" he says, rolling a toothpick east to west between his teeth.

Tizzie is turning blue. Rupert is holding Tizzie's head up and blowing in her mouth. But Monroe can't find a way to get the saw in between the table and the wall with Tizzie laying all over it. Finally, Monroe goes outside and jackhammers the wall out so the table will come loose. Tizzie oozes out of her chair onto the big pile of rubble like un-molding a giant Jello.

It takes eight squads men to move Tizzie. They get her head and shoulders on the stretcher, and her legs and feet ooze off the bottom, and then they get her legs back on, and her head and arms jiggle off. So finally Monroe Lamb rigs up a tarpaulin with two poles rolled up in the ends and they hoist her out on the world's biggest stretcher. All this going on while a squads man is trying to hold an oxygen mask over her mouth.

Rupert is scared to jitters. He tries to keep his cool, though. He tells Sammy in that dignified churchy voice how he and Tizzie tried to avoid a scene. They tried hard not to cause trouble. They tried hard to handle this incident quietly. And now look what we've done. The town of Dixon has sirens and lights blazing to glory, and most of the Baptist convention and the whole town is standing out in the street, craning their heads to see Tizzie being sawed out of her seat.

Tizzie comes around for a few seconds when the men hoist her stretcher off the rubble. She opens her eyes and lifts her head toward Sammy, who is as stiff and white as my Aunt Grace's starched shirts, and whispers with her last breath before she passes out again, "I'm going to sue."

I pick up the wet paper towels I got to put on Tizzie's face and hand them to Sammy. He's got that glazed look like somebody that's been hypnotized, like he wants to walk out of his body and leave it.

Well, I'd like to say that saving Tizzie Dearstone's life was the high point in my day. But it wasn't. After all the sirens blue-lighted Tizzie and Rupert toward the hospital, and the pilgrims marched back toward the downtown Baptist Church, and everything finally got quiet, Sammy Dedmon sat in the floor staring at the big hole in Pee Wee's Emporium, kicking at the pile of rubble with his big toe. Booger Red would have grabbed a wheelbarrow and a trowel. That's the kind of manager he was.

Anyway, I figure Sammy Dedmon is out of his gourd, so me, Gilbert Grubbs, will take charge. I'll get the cash register emptied and the money counted and over to the bank before four o'clock. I figure there's a big bundle of bucks in the till after all the business we done today.

Surprise. Surprise. Surprise. I can't find but $38.42. I look under the money tray and on the floor and on the counter and in the emptied garbage can, but they ain't but $38.42 anyway I count it. I go over to the place on the floor where Sammy is sitting cross-legged and green around the gills, and I show him the money. Only $38.42.

Well, Sammy jumps up quick and says, "Where's Cherry Berry? Ask Cherry. Maybe she's cleared the register and taken the money down to the Dixon National."

I tell Sammy I ain't seen Cherry the whole time we're saving Tizzie Dearstone from Pee Wee's new swivel chair and table and it ain't likely she's done the banking.

Now picture this. Sammy looks right past me at something and I turn around. There's Cherry Berry standing white-faced and glazed like she's a zombie walking out of a graveyard. She's been crying in the girls' bathroom all this time. I'm thinking right about now I should make my move on Cherry. Johnny Frizzell always says, "Catch 'em at their lowest point."

Then Sammy comes over and waves the money at her, asking where's the rest of the money from all the hamburgers we sold today?

Money? What Money? Cherry can't talk about the money. All she can say is that Johnny Frizzell doesn't love her anymore. How is she going to live without Johnny? What is she going to tell her parents when they find out she's knocked up? What is she going to do now?

"No money? No Money?" Sammy shouts in Cherry's face. Then, Sammy tells Cherry to hang up her apron and turn in her uniform. She's fired!

Cherry starts bawling again and runs back into the girls' bathroom. We hear the door slam and the lock snap like a clap of thunder. I think about Cherry's situation now and I can hear Johnny Frizzell whispering in my ear, "Gilbert, run like hell!"

Sammy grabs hold of the counter and looks up at me with a wild, flat face, like Mr. Whipple pressed against a glass window. "Do you think we should call Norma Gentry, Gilbert? What do you think? What do you think about calling Norma Gentry, Gilbert?"

I say, "Yes, Sammy. That's a good idea. You ought to call Norma."

Call Norma Gentry, the dufus says. Monday might have been a different story if we'd had Norma Gentry here. Call Norma Gentry? Hell, ain't that what I told him to do in the first place? I tell Sammy he'd better notify old lady Duncan, too. She'll spit a squealing worm when she finds out there's a hole in the Emporium wall big enough to see the whole town of Dixon.

Just as I get the squealing worm picture in my mind, I look up and there's old lady Duncan and Norma Gentry staring through the open wall looking like the Grandma Bobsy Twins with purple hair, rouged cheeks, lap dews dangling on their collars, and little square pocketbooks dangling on their wrists.

When old lady Duncan fired Sammy Dedmon, he was standing on top of the Dempsey Dumpster behind the Emporium, tearing through bags of garbage. Potato peels and dirty napkins falling through his fingers. Mustard stains and grease spots all over his clothes. Searching for the green bags of money which old lady Duncan explained to him, standing there with her hands on her hips, he had done fried up and fed to his customers.

Seems that Pee Wee's old cash register got so full of money it wouldn't shut, so Cherry had been rolling up the bills and laying them on the meat tray in the cooler. Said it was the only safe place she could think of. Told you she's dumb as a coal bucket, didn't I? Anyway, Sammy Dedmon picked up the meat tray with the money and sent it all through the grinder. The most expensive damned burgers ever served from Pee Wee's grill.

I won't ever forget Sammy Dedmon standing on top of that garbage, porky pig drawn against the sky, the sun going down pinky cheeked over Dixon. I reckoned I felt right sorry for him. But just for a second.

Then I think about how it's going to be when old lady Duncan makes me manager of the Emporium. Who else can she turn to? Herman Little ain't worked but one year. He don't know his head from his rear-end. Johnny Frizzell ain't going to give up his nights off. Norma Gentry is old as a granny woman. That leaves me, Gilbert Grubbs, Junior, thinking about wearing a yellow power tie and a blue suit and growing a mustache and getting my shoes shined. Somehow, the picture of Booger Red comes to mind, working at the grill in his overalls and a white undershirt, sweat drops dangling off his beard. I come to my senses. I'll wear my best suit coat and some blue jeans.

I practice real hard what I'll say to everybody working for me. I see Cherry Berry begging for her job back. I'll have to tell her that beauty ain't nothing without responsibility. That's why it's her fault she's knocked up. I'll tell Norma Gentry she's old as Methuselah. She'd be no use on a doomsday. Make her feel bad. Even an old woman's got to be kept in her place, and I ain't having no trouble out of her. And Johnny Frizzell? I picture telling him to get his butt to work on time for a change. After all, we got five hundred hungry Baptists to feed again tomorrow and if anybody gets fired, it ain't gonna be me. I run a movie of it behind my eyes.

That ain't the way the movie plays. Picture this. Tuesday morning early. Me and Herman Little and Johnny Frizzell, him still puffy under the eyes and sagging about the shoulders, all of us standing behind the counter in the Emporium. A big black tarpaulin pinned over the hole in the wall. Old lady Duncan's flour sack hips swinging into the Emporium. She's decked in a white apron and purple sneakers to match her purple hair and toting a grocery bag clinking with kitchen utensils. Behind her comes the purple shadow, Norma Gentry. Norma's face is bright as a dime that's swallowed a gold dollar.

First, old lady Duncan gathers us in front of the grill for a prayer. Herman is snickering behind me. I reach around and pinch his soft belly. After the Amen, she sterns up. "Things are going to be different around here from now on. Meet your new manager." She lays her fingers on Norma Gentry's shoulder.

It's a pin drop quiet moment until Herman backs into a metal pan of lettuce and it crashes, then rumbles across the floor. Johnny Frizzell yawns like he don't give a damn. He's an artist. He knows how to fake it.

Norma runs her fingers across the grill. Holds them up to the light. Sucks air between her teeth. She growls at Herman to clean up his mess. "You Gilbert," she says. "Cleaning duty tonight. Better get out of that suit." Then she picks up a knife and walks toward Johnny Frizzell. She whispers something in his ear, then jabs the knife toward his crotch. He straightens up fast and heads for the meat cooler.

A strange voice comes out of Norma. "Get to work, you turkeys," she screams at me and Herman. "You're on the clock!"

Norma's voice is a giant gong vibrating through the Emporium. It fades to a loud ringing deep inside my ears and then to a jarring inside my brain. Yeah. Norma's voice sounds like the crack of doom.

Me and My Mean Sister Mary Lee

Me and my sister, Mary Lee, we're mean as a two-headed snake. Mean like tacks in a chair. We're mean like a sharp knife. Meaner than a jail can hold us. Mrs. Bean living upstairs in our project tells us so. Mrs. Bean says she's going to cut out the rocks we got in our chests for hearts and make rock soup. But we got pebble hearts. Our hearts make a broth too thin for sopping biscuits. Mrs. Bean says she's going to turn us in to the sheriff, but we're meaner than the old men they got down in the Dixon County Jail looking out the bars in the alley. Looking down like dying birds.

Mrs. Bean says our Mama should have left us on some mean man's back step when we was born. We need a heavy hand to bring us up. Mrs. Bean says our Mama too puny lipped to bring up twin girls with shiny devil eyes. Mrs. Bean says Mama is too sugary, too slow like molasses talking to me and Mary Lee. "Noooowwww girrrrrlssss. Don't you be throooowwww-nnn rocks through Mrs. Bean's winders." Mrs. Bean is mocking Mama's voice. Twisting her butt like Mama when she's talking.

Mama says back to Mrs. Bean, "Don't you be mocking me, you fat old cow. You leave my babies alone. They are only nine. They are too little to harm anybody."

Old Mrs. Bean says, "Humppff." Tough love is what me and my sister Mary Lee needs to dull our meanness. She is cussing all the way back up her steps.

Me and Mary Lee don't like Mrs. Bean. She and old man Bean with his shirt off and his big belly hanging over his pants and him with a beer can in his hand all the time. Sitting on that fat brown couch upstairs on the back landing, and the fan blowing him while Mrs. Bean is washing her clothes out of that old wringer washer and a big tub up there over our back porch. All crowded.

Mrs. Bean is washing them clothes up a storm. Rinsing them in the big tub of water. Sending them out the wringer flat as pancakes.

She is hanging up her clothes on the line strung up between the posts on her back porch. Hanging them in a certain way, studying how to do it with her tongue wiggling like a worm out the corner of her mouth.

First, she is pinning old man Bean's socks on top of her flower blouse, and pinning his work pants over top the seam of her flower dress, and then she is hanging her old man's blue work shirts upside down so they don't wrinkle, and she don't waste space and she don't waste pins. Then she is hanging up more of old man Bean's pants.

Old man Bean is working at Dixon's Truck Stop out on Highway 11-E. Changing tires. Changing oil. Bean smells like diesel trucks. Like burnt grease. Mrs. Bean, she is washing that grease out of his work clothes, hanging them up like they made of silk. Old man Bean's legs and arms drip, drip, drip, drip. Every day, right on me and Mary Lee cutting paper dolls out of Sears and Roebuck and coloring them with crayons. Making them pretty. Down on our back porch, drip, drip, drip, drip, drip, drip. Right on our heads. Me and Mary Lee moving out of our only spot of shade out in the hot sun and it a trillion degrees out where the dry blades of grass eeching our legs and eeching our arms. It so hot our skin turning purple. Ain't nothing to do but pull out our smelly mattress in the yard and jump up and down, jump up and down.

Mary Lee smells like barbecued potato chips. She is eating a bag all the time, chomp, chomp, chomp, chomp. She is filling up her empty bag with little rocks she picks out of the grass and throws them up at Mrs. Bean's clothes trying to get the rocks to catch in old man Bean's pants pockets and shirt pockets that have been dripping our paper dolls. Then I get me some BIG rocks and help her throw.

Mrs. Bean comes out on her landing and squints down at us with her hand shading her eyes. "You mean girl. You and that Mary Lee. You done busted our winder throwing them rocks up here."

Old man Bean, he comes out on the landing in his underwear with his hairy navel staring down like a big dark eye. He shakes his fist at us. Says he is going to have the project manager run us off. Ain't had no peace since we moved in here, and that's been two weeks and one day ago. Get on back to Morgan City. That's what old man Bean says. What are we doing here in Dixon for anyway?

Old man Bean says me and Mary Lee ain't nothing but a torment.

Says our Mama done named us wrong. Hell and Damnation. That is the right names for twin devils. Two mop heads running on skinny handles. Running every which way. So me and Mary Lee, we giggle with our hands over our mouths. Then we go suck a purple Popsicle. Gonna get a big sticky ring around our mouths. Gonna press purple sugar lips over the Beans' front winders when they ain't looking out. That is Mary Lee's notion.

Me and Mary Lee, we don't like old man Bean. He is on shift work. Coming and going all hours. Waking us up two times already in the middle of the night rattling his old junk car in the project parking lot, and it no muffler on. Roaring like a beast. He is stomping up them metal steps to his home clanking his big feet like he's marching inside a metal drum. Then me and Mary Lee, we done awake and rubbing our eyes. Mama gone to the Cozy Dozy on the night shift, sewing baby clothes.

Well, what we going to do with no TV to watch and us awake? Mary Lee says we got nothing to do but make the Beans mad, pecking up on their ceiling with the broom handle right under the Bean bed. Peck, peck, peck, peck, peck, peck. We take turns. Me pecking. Then Mary Lee.

First though, we wait till old man Bean gets in bed. Then Mr. Bean, he and Mrs. Bean go to shaking and rattling the bed. That bed is romping all over the thin floor like a bucking bronco. Old Man Bean is grunting like a rodeo horse. We giggle in the dark with our hand over our mouths. We know they doing nasty stuff. Then, old man Bean and Mrs. Bean start snoring like that giant and his big wife.

After they snore, we start with the broom pecking on the ceiling to get them waking up. After the broom, Mary Lee gets Mama's big dish pan out of the sink and Mama's big spoons and we play drums, loud as we can, jumping up and down on the bed. Mary Lee jumping on the head end and I jumping on the knees. We start shouting, screaming, and beating our drums right under the Bean bed. We go a long time.

Old man Bean is getting his head down on the floor cussing us. His voice muffles down like the ceiling is talking. Then we beat the drums and beat on the ceiling with the broom handle right where his head is talking down. Old man Bean comes stomping down the tinny stairs in his underwear and banging on our door. BANG. BANG. BANG.

BANG. BANG. Our old door rattles on the hinges like it's going to bust down.

Old man Bean shouting and banging. "I'm going to tear down your door, and bite you in two. Snap you like toothpicks!"

Its 3:00 a.m. when Mama comes off the night shift from Cozy Dozy. She's dead tired and all hunched over from sewing baby clothes. She sees old man Bean naked in his underwear, banging on our door. She comes in and sees me and Mary Lee crying and rubbing our eyes and screaming at old man Bean. Him cussing a fit. I get good and scared, but that Mary Lee she ain't scared of nothing. She is just pretending.

Mama and old man Bean shout and cuss right up in each other's faces. "You leave my precious little girls alone. You monster man, standing outside our door with your skinny legs sticking out your underwear."

Old man Bean cusses back. Then Mama and old man Bean go to jabbing each other on the shoulder. Mama comes in to call the police, dialing 9-1-1. Old man Bean pushes Mama inside trying to find me and Mary Lee. We hide behind the bedroom door, crying and peeking out that crack above the hinges.

The neighbors come in from all over the project. Rosa Rosemond on the end. She got six girls that won't play with us. Says we too mean. Old Mrs. Pickle, scooting on her arthritis feet. Manford Stanhopper, the honey-dipper. Sucks out cesspools for the county, part time. He is stinking like poopy. They all crowd in our little apartment. Talking all at a time in everybody's faces.

The police, they come with the screaming cars and the lights going blue in the night, and find old man Bean and Mama fist-fighting. He done knocked Mama down on the couch, making her nose bleed. The police say they going to take old man Bean off to jail again for bothering two little skinny girls, and him banging on our door and his big hairy belly scaring us to death and him beating up our tired Mama. Lewd and lass-vicious behavior. And this is the second time he done it. The police say they going to keep him longer in jail this time.

The police gently patting Mama on the shoulder, poor old Mama working so hard and scared to death for her little girls. "What a hell of a life," Mama says to them. The police write down Mama's words.

"My man done gone off with some big wide woman. Gone to Texas or California, don't know which. Me and the girls move out of our nice little house in a nice neighborhood into this project with all these low class, trashy people, and me working night shift at Cozy Dozy sewing baby clothes until my fingers numb to the bone, trying to keep bread in our bellies." Mama cries like Niagara Falls now. "Ain't they no justice against that child abuser? That old man Bean?"

The police look over at me and Mary Lee crying and shivering like we cold. We done hid the broom and the drum before they come.

Mrs. Bean, she coming down now with her head full of pink curlers, them soft twist kind. She's a fat old woman in her skinny night gown and they is freckles on her chest where her big boobies hang loose under her gown. She is crying, wringing her tissue around her finger and begging the policeman to let her old man go. But the police pay her no mind. The police make old man Bean put on his clothes and go to the Dixon County Jail.

The neighbors down on the end of the project, Rosa Rosemond and her girls Heather, Ginger, Gina, Babbs, Trina, Tina, all friends of the Beans, they are taking Mrs. Bean down to the jail, and after she visits inside for her time, she stands in the alley crying and holding up her hands trying to reach her old man looking out the bars of the Dixon County Jail. Him crying too, and trying to reach down to her. But they is glass over the bars. Old Rosa Rosemond tells us all about this after they come home from the jail and it's five o'clock a.m. and Mama too scared and nervous to go to bed, that Roza comes into our apartment telling Mama about old man Bean crying like a dying bird, making Mama feel bad for old man Bean. Her girls all twirling her skirt tail.

But Mama tells Rosa Rosemond that a strumpet and her six girls with all different fathers ain't going to make her feel bad about old man Bean after what he done. Scaring us to death and us little bitty things, all alone at night in the dark mean world, and Mama gone to work and she not protecting us.

Me and Mary Lee are going to wait for old man Bean. He is coming out of jail in two days. We got nothing to do. Mary Lee says we going to throw rocks down on some cars driving through the underpass out on Wylie Dixon Highway, but it's too hot to walk out there now. We waiting for Mama to go to work. Waiting for the cool weather.

Mary Lee says while we're waiting for the cars, she's studying on something better to do. So now we get our flip flops and our jelly shoes out of the closet, and we sprinkle the kitchen floor thick with Mama's good Avon talcum powder that smells like roses, and we skate all over the floor on our hands and our feet, bumping and giggling. Bumping and giggling. First, me. And then, Mary Lee. I get my elbows up.

After we get done skating, Mary Lee gets a notion about doing something to them Barbie Doll Rosemonds living on the end. Maybe that old Rosa Rosemond, too. Mary Lee whispers her plan in my ear. Tickling my ear with her mean whispering.

Killing Oranges

I read in a murder mystery magazine at the back of Ziggie's Newsstand that I can kill my husband by driving a nail in his ear while he is asleep. Then, I must pull it out. No one will find out. The ear does not bleed, so there is no evidence. No blood. That is important to me, because I hate the sight of blood.

An icicle will work as well as a nail. The evidence melts into a puddle and evaporates. Tricky, though, because icicles are unpredictable. The icicle could melt in my sweaty hand if I hesitate too long. Too long before winter. There are long, sharp icicles frozen to the guttering during January.

I can kill him through his eyeball, too. Pull back the lid and drive a wire through the corner of the eye, through the open socket, carefully, carefully, into the soft tissue of the brain. Make sure it is a fine, strong wire. Long and thin. *Mother's pearl hatpin*? Make sure I have steady hands, determination, concentration. Make sure he is doped into a deep sleep so he will lie still, cooperate. Be warned about the blood. A drop or two at least, the magazine says.

I am sure now that I must kill him with a nail. I am used to nails. Daddy was a carpenter. He built houses and banks, and buildings for companies. Daddy drank, too, and hammered nails. I am used to the pound, pound, pounding of nails in planks.

I am used to the smell of liquor, rough beard like sandpaper on my face, eyes swimming through hazy puddles above me. But never the blood in beads along the floor where I run to find Mother. *Mother*?

Daddy would not build for Mother, even if the doors fell from their hinges. Stubborn.

I consider buying a gun, but there will be evidence. Papers to sign, the gun salesman, squint-eyed, attentive, a sponge soaking up every characteristic of my face, remembering my nervous twitching, my silly questions, my excuses. With a gun, there will be blood.

The body? Getting rid of it, and the gun? Too much mess. Too risky. Too nerve-racking.

Perhaps I will manage the gun? I will wait until he is asleep, put a pillow over his head, point, pull the trigger? I will be scared. He will not drink enough of the liquor I have laced with sleeping medicine. I am standing over him. I will close my eyes a second to gather courage, and he will wake up, suddenly, grab the gun from my sweaty hands. Shoot me. My blood all over the floor and the walls. All over Daddy. He will tell them he killed me in self-defense. They will believe Daddy.

No, I am smarter than Mother. Much smarter.

I find EAR in the encyclopedia and with my husband's carpenter's pencil, I draw twenty-two ears along a two-by-four from a pile of lumber he is saving. I practice hammering nails into the wooden ears late in the afternoons at the back of the garage. I use my husband's workbench, his nails, his hammer. He is a carpenter. He builds houses.

The girls are playing outdoors in their little rubber swimming pool. I hear them giggling between the pounds of my hammer. Their giggling distracts me and I hit my thumb. *There is blood on the plank. Drops of my blood on the white plank.*

"What are you doing, Mommy? Why are you hammering nails?" They have found me at the back of the garage sucking the hurt from my thumb.

"I am building a new dog house for Trixie," I tell them, tasting salt. They believe me.

"Can we hammer, too?" They giggle, pulling a ball-peen hammer from their daddy's toolbox.

"NO! NO! NO!" I shout at them. "You must NEVER, NEVER, NEVER hammer nails!"

They cover their ears, look at me. They run away to the pool. I do not understand their eyes, why my little girls look at me that way when I am trying so hard. They do not understand that I have seen him. He does not know that I watch. But I have seen him patting their ruffled swim suits, kissing them, kissing them. At bedtime.

"What in the hell are you nailing up?" he shouts at me.

He is home from work early. I am caught with twenty-two nails, big ones, hammered in, some crooked, some straight, into his ear. He surprises me. I jump. But I have steadier nerves than Mother.

"Hammering nails is a new therapy we've been trying in our group.

Releases tension, helps me to focus. I feel better already." I smile up at him as he studies me, studies my intentions nailed up twenty-two different ways.

"Don't ruin all that good lumber. It's damned expensive." His eyes jerk over me, cold, like he is looking at me through ice. "You're damned expensive."

He always says this when I mention my therapy group.

Mother made cookies. That was her therapy. She found the recipe in a ladies' magazine. Frustration Cookies. A simple recipe of flour and loads of butter, like shortbread. You pound them, the recipe says. Pound, pound, pound them. The more you pound, the better they taste. The more you pound, the better you feel.

Mother let me help. We pounded the dough, together, on a wooden board. The dough gets lighter and whiter. Never black and blue like you would expect. Daddy eats them all. He smiles. We feel better.

He is inside the kitchen. I hear the top pop off a beer can, the sound of the TV comes out the screen door. The rattle of newspapers. The smell of baloney and cheese. I can see everything he does, even when I am not looking.

Mother believed in therapy. She went to assertiveness training, but she never learned how to say, *NO!* I have learned to watch.

Learning to drive nails is not easy. I have tried all sizes. Thin and long is best, the magazine says. But they bend easily. I try big and little hammers from his tool chest. I balance them in my hand.

Daddy says the art of driving nails is in the flick of the wrist. He tries to teach me, but I do not want to learn.

My wrist hurts. I take a break. I eat a navel orange.

I should not be hammering wood, I tell myself, looking at the navel orange I am eating. Peeling and eating it, a lobe at a time. Peeling it with my finger in its ear. I am all wrong. The ear is soft and spongy, not hard, not like pounding planks.

I go to the grocery to buy navel oranges. The checkout man makes a joke. "Got a craving for navels, huh?"

He winks at me like he knows. His eyes follow the ruffles bouncing on my little girls' dresses out the electric doors. *He bears careful watching.*

I take home two 10-pound sacks of navel oranges. Nothing else.

I kill them all. One after the other, pounding them through their soft, rubbery ears, pounding into their soft brains with a flick of my wrist, with my hammer and a long, thin nail, with their ears turned up to me out of the white pillow.

The magazine did not tell me he would jerk like a live wire fallen into water, that he would jump and jerk and then fall into a naked heap like a rumpled blanket on top of the bed.

Too late. The fifth of Johnny Walker is empty on the bed stand. I make sure. I put on my clothes.

I keep the girls in the kitchen. I give them a bowl of Cheerios and milk. "You can eat supper in peace tonight. You can sleep in peace tonight," I tell them. They stare at me, silently, from behind their bowls. Their eyes float on the milk. Their spoons are pointing. Pointing.

"I tried to get him awake," I tell the ambulance driver. "I shook him. He would not wake up. He drank the bottle dry. All at once. Down, down in big swallows. *Mother? Mother? Mother?*

The ambulance driver chews gum with his mouth open. He nods without looking at me. Writes on a clipboard. *Possible alcohol poisoning.* I watch his writing out of the corner of my eye.

The ambulance driver and another man bring in a plank bed on wheels. He is very still. His head is crooked on his pillow. His eyes are open, floating up white like dead minnows.

The magazine is right. There is nary a drop of blood.

Jack Mooneyham is Going to Hell

Jack Mooneyham is going to hell. I know because Mama says so. Mama has it on good authority from Mary Mildred McMurtry who certainly has first-hand evidence against Jack Mooneyham since she lives down the hill from the Mooneyhams' house and has observed Jack Mooneyham often enough in the act of his sinfulness. Well, not exactly right in the act. But pretty nearly in the act. And the funny thing is, Jack Mooneyham doesn't even know that we know that he's about to go to hell in a hand basket if he doesn't straighten up.

Mama says that Mary Mildred McMurtry has not *spied*, mind you, but *observed* Jack Mooneyham coming and going from Hattie and Mollie Bingham's house, even before dark sets in. Now Hattie and Mollie Bingham are two old spinster sisters who live below Mary Mildred's house, and just as likely as the sun will set, why, that Jack Mooneyham lights out for the Binghams' every Monday night, faithful and true, after milking is done, and there is Hattie waiting at her back door wearing her Sunday dress and smiling at Jack like he is Santa Claus with a sack full of toys, and Jack all blushed up like he is still in puberty and him over sixty years old, the dirty old man, and Hattie nearly that old herself. Mama says it's unfortunate that Mary Mildred must live right between these sinful people.

Well, when Mama told me that Jack Mooneyham is going to hell in a hand basket I said, "Mama, how can that be? Jack Mooneyham is a *good* man. He stays home and sees to his mama and daddy, forsaking marriage all these years just to take care of them. He does all the farming now that his old daddy is down with arthritis so bad in his hips. Why, he keeps up that big house of theirs, always hammering and nailing and painting, and him a member, longstanding, of New Ebenezer Presbyterian Church. Now, I ask you Mama, how can a good man like that go to hell?"

Mama is canning a run of tomatoes, stuffing them plump and red into the top of a quart jar, and she switches her head toward me and says, "Jack Mooneyham forn-i-cates."

I run all the thou-shall-nots through my head, counting down the list of all ten of them, and forn-i-cates doesn't ring a bell.

"What does forn-i-cates mean, Mama?"

"I suppose you're old enough to know such things by now," says Mama. "It means doing family duty when you are not married and sanctified by God to be doing family duty. And Jack Mooneyham has been forn-i-cating with Hattie Bingham, right under Mollie's nose."

"I just don't believe it. He's such a good man. That's what everybody in the church says." I shake away the vision of red horns growing out of Jack Mooneyham's head. I try not to think of hell's flames, seven times hotter than fire, burning him for eternity.

Mama cans in a nice round, red tomato that looks like a heart. Then Mama tells me how she's heard Mary Mildred talk about Jack Mooneyham, the rake, carrying on with Hattie Bingham for years, but she didn't believe a word of it. Mama says she thought it was just gossip until Monday night when she observed firsthand what Jack Mooneyham has been up to. "Well, I tell you girl. I've seen for myself."

"Mama, you didn't watch them having family duty? I mean, forn-i-cating?"

"No, no, of course I didn't exactly watch them doing anything, but I saw plenty of smoke, and where there's smoke there's a fire lit. I hate to admit this, but Mary Mildred must be telling the truth after all."

Mama says that a mature man like Jack Mooneyham ought to have sense to keep his unspeakable doings a secret. Why should he make such a show of himself now, after all these years? Right in broad daylight? Mama stuffs tomatoes into the clean quart canning jars while she stands by the sink and tells me what she saw and heard at Mary Mildred's house.

"Mary Mildred invited me and Elizabeth Godsey over last Monday night to help her break a bushel of runner beans," says Mama. "We're all sitting on Mary Mildred's back porch in the swing, breaking beans up a storm and remarking on how well the gardens have done this year. You know, we've had a bumper crop of tomatoes, the ones I'm canning here, and the runner beans and corn have never done better, and well, we looked up the hill to the back of the Mooneyham house, and there was Jack swinging out the screen door wearing Sunday trousers and his hair all slicked and it a Monday night. Jack lopes down the pathway and goes across Mary Mildred's pasture, and around the edge of her barnyard, and on down to Hattie and Mollie Bingham's back door.

"Mary Mildred leans her head in toward us and says, *Now, observe that Hattie will come out on the back porch and greet him all smiling and tee-hee-heeing and wringing her hands like a wet mop.*

"Sure enough," says Mama, "There stood Hattie in her good dress, the blue one with pale yellow cornflowers in the background, smoothing her grey hair back up into a bun, love-twitching all over. Jack was twisting his hat around and around in his hands and stepping from one foot to the other like he was barefooted on hot rocks. I tell you it was perfectly disgusting. Poor Elizabeth Godsey never does notice a thing unless you stick her nose right in it. She says, *How long has this been going on?*

"Mary Mildred picks up a hand full of beans and says calm as a cucumber, *Nineteen years.*

"Elizabeth Godsey dropped a newspaper full of strings and ends right into the bean pot and had to fish them all out.

"*Nineteen years? Good Lord!* says Elizabeth.

"And Mary Mildred says without breaking stride in her bean breaking, *That's right. Nineteen years, gone March.*

"Elizabeth Godsey had her mouth open wide enough to swallow the Sluder River Bridge, so Mary Mildred says, *Elizabeth, dear, close your mouth. You're catching flies.*

"And Elizabeth says, *Good Lord. Jack Mooneyham's soul is in perilous danger. Now doesn't that bother you just a little bit, Mary Mildred?*

"Mary Mildred, who is more calloused to life than Elizabeth ever will be, shakes her head in that funny way she does. You know, girl, like it is dancing all by itself, and she says, *He seems right pleased about going to hell, if you ask me. Got so, he doesn't even care if anybody sees him going down there. He used to wait until dark. I've observed him from right behind my kitchen curtains, moving down this hill in the shadows, stopping and looking this way and that, and then sneaking like a love-thief into Hattie's kitchen, all these years! Now he goes down there when it's still daylight for the world to behold.*

"*His poor mother,* says Elizabeth. *Poor old Mrs. Mooneyham. What must she think of her son?*

"I saw Mary Mildred's eyes gleaming and I knew she was getting ready to let loose on Elizabeth. Sure enough she said, *She must be reconciled by now, I should think. After all, they've done it 951 times.*

"You could have knocked Elizabeth out of her seat with a fly swat. You know how quiet she is. She actually screamed, *Good Lord have mercy. 951 times?*

"You know Mary Mildred. She wouldn't get shook up if you put her in a butter churn. She holds up her fingers toward Elizabeth, *If you count up nineteen years of Monday nights, not counting holidays, you come up with 951 times. That is, counting last Monday night. And 952 if you count tonight.*

"That Mary Mildred always did have a head for figures," says Mama. "So we didn't dispute a word of what she said."

"Forget about the math, Mama. What happened next?" I say.

"Then Elizabeth brought up a fine point, I believe, when she said, *Why does he go there only on Monday nights? Now doesn't that strike you both as being odd?*

"But you know that Mary Mildred always has an answer for everything. She says, *You're a married woman yourself, Elizabeth Godsey. You must know that every man has a different call of nature.*

"What is a different call of nature?" I say.

"Never mind about that." Mama waves her tomato juice hand at me.

"Does Mary Mildred have a lot of brothers? She knows a lot about men?"

Mama drops a tomato on the floor and stoops over to pick it up. "Just listen to the story, girl. Where was I? Oh, yes. Elizabeth says, *It still seems right odd to me. You'd think they would just do the decent thing and get married.*

"Mary Mildred says, *I understand, Elizabeth, that some people find living on the edge of danger more thrilling and sexually sustaining. Even if they have to burn in hell for it.*

"That was a naughty thing for Mary Mildred to say, and I certainly agreed when Elizabeth called her a hussy. Elizabeth's face turned red as a beet. She shook all over, and said that Mary Mildred should certainly have told her about this sooner, rather than later. What a nasty shock. Elizabeth said she was always the last to know these things.

But, Mary Mildred said it was worth waiting nineteen years to tell Elizabeth. Now, Elizabeth couldn't dismiss her in that self-righteous, prudish way of hers," said Mama.

I am about to ask Mama what sexually sustaining means when she says, "You know, daughter dear, these tomatoes look so pretty in the can, they're all round and red, they're evenly sized, and they have a good, firm texture. I believe I'll enter a jar or two in the Dixon County Fair. I'm sure these tomatoes will be judged perfect!"

"Oh Mama. Forget those tomatoes for a minute and tell me what happened next."

"We finished the beans. Enough for twenty quarts and one pint. And Elizabeth Godsey finished her part without saying another word. There's going to be trouble between her and Mary Mildred. I can just feel it," says Mama.

"I mean, what happened with Jack Mooneyham?"

"Oh, well. He went inside the house with Hattie. And you had better not be thinking about the rest, young lady." Mama looks up at me over the tops of her bifocals and screws a can lid tight on the jar of tomatoes.

"Mama? Didn't you get your two cents worth into that conversation with Mary Mildred and Elizabeth?"

"All I had to say was that I'm sure glad that Hattie Bingham is too old to get P.G." Mama puts her cans of tomatoes in the cooker and turns on the heat.

I think to myself, "What about Hattie's older sister Mollie? Wonder what she does to occupy herself while Jack Mooneyham is loving her sister in their great big four-poster bed?" I can just imagine Mollie going about her kitchen chores, putting away the supper dishes, wiping off the kitchen table, hanging the dishrag neatly over the dish drainer, sweeping out the crumbs, and such. Humming a little tune perhaps. Maybe watching the news on TV, like nothing at all is amiss.

Then I think to myself, "Hattie Bingham and Jack Mooneyham? Together?" It's easier to picture Scarlet O'Hara and Rhett Butler, locked in a hot embrace. After all, I've seen *Gone With the Wind* thirty-eight times. Rhett is about to join the fighting. He and Scarlet are standing on a high ridge, the red glow of Atlanta burning far in the background. Scarlet is molded to the curve of Rhett's powerful chest. Rhett's arms go around Starlet's waist and shoulders. She feels the hard muscles of his thighs against her legs, the buttons of his coat pressing into her soft breasts, his mustache tickling her lips and his mouth pressing hotly, gently down on hers. She is weak, limp, helpless against this newfound longing. As Rhett begs Scarlet to kiss him, to love him, he tells Scarlet she will be sending a soldier to his death with beautiful memories. Rhett bends Starlet's body backward and his lips travel down her throat…. Now, that's passion.

I tell you, imagining Hattie and Jack in a passionate embrace? Why, Hattie has a wrinkly neck and large-knuckled farm hands. Every hair on Hattie's head is grey, but she's got a shock of black hair on her upper lip. Hattie doesn't even smell, well, you know, sexy. She smells like cooking spices and flour, not all sweetly scented like Scarlet O'Hara. What's worse is that Hattie has a bulge under the waist of her dress like a hard round ball where a flat tummy should be, and she hasn't even had babies. Well, as far as I know anyway. No sir. Hattie Bingham is not the kind of woman you can picture locked in a passionate embrace with a man, not even an old man like Jack Mooneyham who has stocky legs and thinning hair. The idea is revolting.

Mama takes a can of tomatoes out of the boiler. A cloud of steam escapes into the kitchen. The tomatoes look like red hearts boiling in a jar, boiling without bursting, hissing, throbbing.

"Mama," I say, "If Jack Mooneyham is going to hell for forn-i-cating, what do you reckon God will do with Hattie Bingham?"

Mama is wrapping a towel around the hot cans of tomatoes, hearts beating in darkness under their blanket. Mama gets her face all twisted into a question mark, and after a while she says, "Why, lordy, girl! It takes two to forn-i-cate, now don't it?"

"I guess so." I think of how I feel hugging my pillow at night, getting all swimmy headed playing like I'm Scarlet O'Hara, my lips bunched together with Rhett Butler's, my chest feels rosy.

Mama's face goes peculiar, something between a smile and a frown. Her upper lip twitches at the corner. "Just you wait until I remind Mary Mildred that Hattie Bingham is riding to hell in the same hand basket. Mary Mildred will be mad as a hornet she didn't think of it first."

A Wind Among the Stars

When Mary Margaret Jenkins was twelve years old and had the common sense of a chicken, she got it into her birdy brain to drive her brother Elroy's car, a 1952 Ford, a big high-off-the-ground boxy automobile with lots of glass and chrome. It sat beneath a lean-to under the Gilly tree shining like a trophy, and whenever Mary Margaret looked at Elroy's car, she got a great senseless passion to drive. After Mary Margaret's driving escapade across the mountains toward Asheville, the neighbors told the story over and over, saying she had the same brainless craving that a chicken gets to cross the road. Wasn't it a god's shame her parents had the burden of her to raise, and her daddy the minister of the church.

Elroy had worked hard to buy the car, worked three years, before his sixteenth birthday, mowing lawns, helping farmers put up hay, milking cows for neighbors of a summertime when they took a notion to visit relations in far off places, or go down to Myrtle Beach for a week. He cut tobacco, or hauled melons to market, or slaughtered pigs, earning a few dollars along.

Elroy even took eggs to the store for old Mrs. Tremble who lived five miles back up Tremble Holler. Elroy rode his bike part way and walked the rutty hills of Tremble Holler the remainder, coming and going. When he delivered Mrs. Tremble's egg money and basket, she'd lay a nickel in his sweaty palm like it was gold and say, "Elroy, you've got the makings of a fine man."

Elroy never turned down an opportunity to earn money, and good boy that he was, dropped every sweaty nickel and dime into a peanut butter jar that he kept on the shelf over his closet. He kept a ledger under the jar in which he recorded his profits. June 3, 1960. Mrs. Tremble. 5 cents.

Mary Margaret turned out the exact opposite of Elroy. Aunt Leona Jenkins first recognized Mary Margaret's sad affliction when Mary Margaret lay in her crib one week old. "Looky. That Mary Margaret is the spittle of her Grandma Lissie on the Monroe side of the family. Lord. She won't be worth a dime."

All of Grandma Lissie's posterity knew the queer stories about her. As a child, Lissie was flighty as a blue jay, out in the garden one minute and in the barnyard the next. She could be out in the field picking seedpods from the nightshade to fashion dolls, a girl with a skirt and a boy in pants, and a second later, popping honeysuckle onto her tongue out by the fence row. Lissie was a fidget. She made everybody dizzy headed.

By the time she was eight, everybody knew that Lissie Monroe wouldn't amount to a hill of beans. She couldn't keep her mind on a thing for one minute, unless it was something useless. Lissie stood for time-on-end examining her face in stump water, noticing how the water-mirror threw her face upon the dark rotten stump, wondering if there was some portent to the vision. Lissie examined clouds endlessly, watched them change from elephants to tigers, then to sheep, studying how the wind could draw things in the sky, wishing she could have that magic.

As a child, she swung on the grapevine in the holler, out across the pond, and back into the woods, like a pendulum, hour upon hour, and never tired of seeing how the patterns of her skirt could arrange shadows upon the surface of the pond, or of counting the circles on the water a jumping bullfrog made. Why could some bullfrogs make more circles than others? When Lissie put such questions to her elders, why, they shook their heads and quietly admitted, "Lissie Monroe is brain-addled."

Lissie managed to find herself a good man, a hard worker. Her daddy, who was a river-bottom farmer, would tell you if he was alive that the Lord works in mysterious ways. He would tell you how hard he prayed for a good man to marry Lissie, to take care of her in her dotage. As it turned out, Lissie married a Jenkins and bore five sons who made a lawyer, a doctor, a banker, and two made preachers.

"Lordy. I don't know how those boys turned out so well and them off Lissie Monroe," people said. They'd tell you about seeing Lissie spending an hour studying ants work in an out of a hole, or coming into church with her milking dress on, smelling of cows and chicken feed, or walking to the store with her shoes on the wrong feet.

"But look here," another would remind, "Them boys' daddy is Millford Jenkins, off them Jenkins over by Greenback. Those boys got the Jenkins' blood."

The Jenkins could put backs to their hoes and make ten bushels of corn to every five their neighbors made. The Jenkins grew the highest tobacco, the most melons, the longest beans. They had seed corn to share and wheat to grind when everybody else's granaries were empty as a beggar's belly.

The Jenkins aunts, uncles and cousins never tired of pointing out the resemblance between Mary Margaret and her Grandma Lissie, the Monroe side of the family. They remembered Mary Margaret lying in her crib, sucking like a milking machine, with her thumb stuck up her nose. Or how, as she grew up, she emptied every drawer in their houses looking for the hidden treasure that only a child born wrong could imagine. The Jenkins pointed out her jack-in-the-box mannerisms, and felt sorry for the burden of Mary Margaret on her family. Mary Margaret, who was ten years old before she stayed still long enough to learn to tie her shoes, was as air-headed and flighty as her Grandma Lissie ever dared to be.

"Mary Margaret, did you fold the towels and washrags out of the clothes basket?" her mama would ask.

And Mary Margaret, who went instead to play with butterflies in the back yard, said, "Mama, why is it the harder I go at catching butterflies, the easier they get away, and when I stand still, why, they come and land on my nose?"

"Mary Margaret, get the dishes out of that rinse water and dry them up. Right now."

Mary Margaret stood with her hands in the water until they were pruny, looking out the kitchen window. "Mama. How do you suppose a hummingbird can beat his wings so fast a body can't see them and stay still at the same time?"

"The blackberries are ripe by the fence row on Mr. Sutton's place. Mary Margaret, go fetch a pan full for a cobbler."

Mary Margaret studied the briars on the vines and a hawk circling overhead while she picked the berries. She studied the tracings in the air that bumblebees make, and how the heat shimmies above the vines. And walking home, she ate out of the berry pan, engrossed with the wonderment of a snake racing down the hill and crawling into its hole. How did it crawl so fast, and it no feet? Wasn't it mole-blind? How did it find its hole?

"Mary Margaret Jenkins. There's nothing but berry stain left in this pan," said her mama. "Where is your mind, girl?"

Mary Margaret's mama stopped giving her chores to do. It was a day's work to keep Mary Margaret out of mischief and her half-grown. She'd bring in an armload of Queen Anne's lace to decorate the churn, and everybody dug at chiggers for a week. Once she brought in a leaf with pretty eggs, and a crop of clothes moths hatched in the closet, ate her mama's wool sweaters to polka-dots and Preacher Jenkins's best winter wool suit to ribbons. On the fifth try, she lost the new tin bucket down the cistern counting the seconds until it hit water, comparing if it took the same seconds each time. She was forbidden near a cooking pot for fear she'd burn the house.

"She's Grandma Lissie to a T," they'd all say, and Mary Margaret let the words roll off her like duck water. Mary Margaret's mind floated in the ethereal, and earthly opinions registered with less weight than the clattering of wind in the trees.

Elroy took after the Jenkins side of the family, a quiet, hardworking boy. During the school year, he ran a paper route, riding his bike for miles around the country roads. Summers, he also mowed, milked, cut and stacked, grubbed, gathered up or spread down, planted, hoed, watered and weeded, reaped, cleared, plowed and readied to plant again.

Elroy neither wasted time talking, nor did he dribble his money away. "You can get a job of work done faster than talking about it," a Jenkins will tell you. He rose long before sun cracked the mountains, and bedded long after moon rise. He never bought new what could be repaired and re-used, he never spent a nickel where a penny would do.

Elroy's father pastored a church circuit in the farming heart of Dixon County, and every member of Hartman's Chapel, and Piney Grove, and Bewley's Chapel knew Preacher Jenkins's son and they offered Elroy all the work he would handle.

"Elroy's head is tied to his hands," Woody Kirk might say to Beamer Colyer, who would nod back, "Yes sir, Elroy's got lard in his elbows."

Elroy could strike a bargain, too. It surprised no one when Elroy bought the used Ford off Bondo Lemmings, paid cash money, and drove the car home. The Ford needed fixing. Elroy put in new gaskets and belts, put a new float in the carburetor, bought a new battery, put in a better clutch, replaced the tail lights, and re-wired the starter.

Mary Margaret put her head into everything Elroy did. "Elroy, how can that carburetor burn gas and the car not burn up? Elroy, how does that crankshaft going round and round like a clock spring, make the wheels go different directions, front wards and backwards? Elroy, why does that Ford need an electric starter when the car runs off gas? Elroy, what's a clutch?"

Like the Jenkins, Elroy was patient and unflappable, slow to anger and good natured toward Mary Margaret. What people remarked to each other about Mary Margaret, they'd never dare say to Elroy's face for they sensed his strange protectiveness of her.

Elroy answered Mary Margaret's questions, best he could, although talking about what he was doing slowed his hands, and her eyes and mouth went everywhere with Elroy's hands. Sometimes they bumped heads under the steering column, or a wheel well, or under the hood.

By summer's end, Elroy had the Ford refitted and ready to drive on a regular basis. Elroy knocked out the dents with a mallet, and painted the car light marine green, bought white-walled retreads, put in a better radio, waxed and polished the chrome. That Ford shined. He built a lean-to under the Gilly tree for covering.

Sometimes on a Sunday afternoon, Elroy took the family for a drive in the Ford. Mary Margaret rode in the front seat wedged between Elroy and their Mama. Preacher Jenkins rode in the back, spread his legs out on the wide back seat, said he wanted to be chauffeured.

Mary Margaret studied the motions of Elroy's hands on the steering wheel. She pondered him releasing the clutch, changing gears, kneading the brake pedal, moderating the gas. Sometimes Elroy's hands were changing gears and steering while his feet worked from the clutch to the brake pedal and back to the gas. Mary Margaret was amazed at how Elroy's hands and feet knew what to do automatically, all the while Elroy remarking on Old Man Higgins's corn, or Nancy and Max Crumley's fine garden, or Harry Luttrell's watermelon patch, and weren't there a thousand of them. How will he ever sell them all?

Elroy's Ford hummed along the highway, trees and sky passing across the windshield, scenes changing, a lifetime of questions flashing by Mary Margaret's eyes. She felt like a millionaire of time, the calm waterwheels of her mind turning puzzlement over puzzlement. If only she could drive the car like Elroy, who looked out the windows and talked while his hands and feet thought about the driving, she could go places and consider a world of questions.

Out of a lull came Mary Margaret's voice. "Elroy. Can I drive?"

On Monday afternoon, Elroy drove to the store for twenty pounds of sugar for Mrs. Jenkins to make a run of grape jelly. Mary Margaret sat upon Elroy's knees and turned the steering wheel while he changed gears. Afterwards, on short trips to the store or the church or over to a neighbor's house, often as not, you'd see Elroy driving with Mary Margaret perched upon his knees before the steering wheel.

"Who'd a thought that gawky girl could keep that big car in the road," people stood out in their yards and pointed when Elroy's Ford went by.

"Lord. Ain't that fine boy, that Elroy, got the patience of a woman?" another neighbor said.

When Mary Margaret mastered the steering, Elroy instructed her on changing gears. He took her out on the flat of a pasture and drove in Z's and S's and in big, wide circles, slowing down and starting up, stopping and going, working the clutch and the brakes while Mary Margaret shifted and steered. Soon, Mary Margaret's shifting synchronized with the clutch down, and the brake up, with the stopping and the going.

One day, Elroy let Mary Margaret drive the Ford by herself. She perched on the edge of the front seat, her quizzical head cocked up to the steering wheel. She stuck out her thumb, pushed the starter button, stretched her legs to the pedals on the floor board, took hold of the steering wheel, and drove.

While Mary Margaret drove mostly in the pasture, Elroy drove greater distances, sometimes taking the Ford as far as Asheville to the Rodeo, or to Newport News to sell a load of tomatoes, or to the Dixon County Fair in late summer. Elroy brought back stories of his trips. But the stories Mary Margaret enjoyed most was Elroy's telling of his trip to the Dixon County Fair, of the great Ferris wheel and his belly falling out from under him, of the gypsy fortune teller and her crystal ball, and of the two-headed calf, one head bawling and the other silent.

He described the smallest man in the world, twenty four inches high, eleven pounds, sitting upon a tiny velvet chair on a table top, his hands and feet small as an infant's.

"Elroy. Could that little man talk?" asked Mary Margaret.

Elroy said he could talk about baseball or the weather same as anybody.

Elroy described the old man, white bearded, who had a baby growing out of his belly where the old man's navel should be, a dead baby, with eyes closed and limp shriveled fists, joined at its waist to the man's body, and the old man standing in a tent, shirtless, cradling what he called a baby boy in his hands.

"Elroy. Is that baby boy the old man's brother or his son?" asked Mary Margaret.

Elroy said the old man called the baby his twin brother, Elmo.

"Elroy. How does that old man know it's a boy, and it only half a baby? And how can that baby be dead and not rotten?"

Elroy said he didn't know, but he'd seen it with his own eyes.

Mary Margaret longed to drive to the Dixon County Fair to see such marvels, to see her reflection in the hall of mirrors, to wind her way through the Labyrinthine, to see Snake Woman with her 30 foot python wrapped around her like a great squirming necklace, to see the largest horse in the world, the biggest rat, the smallest man.

"Elroy. Can I go to the Dixon County Fair?"

Elroy said he didn't see why Mary Margaret couldn't go to the fair someday.

On a bright afternoon in early September, Mary Margaret put on her best dress, backwards, and her best sweater, inside out. She put a box of saltine crackers, a jar of peanut butter, and a pint of her mama's bread and butter pickles in a brown poke, and set off in Elroy's Ford for Dixon.

Mary Margaret's mama was making a jelly roll for Sunday dinner, Elroy was spudding tobacco in Sam Dody's tobacco patch, and Preacher Jenkins had his thumb on Genesis meditating on what a mean-spirited woman Sarah was and how Abraham was a spineless man for allowing Hannah and his own son to be sent to the desert to die. Yes, he would preach on man's impatience with God, his weakness in his faith, and his predilection for betrayal of those who depend most upon his grace.

Even in the quietness of their work, no one heard Elroy's Ford purring out the driveway. Mary Margaret drove toward what she believed to be Dixon, but she turned right handed out of the driveway and instead navigated toward the spiraled mountain road going over Sam's Gap toward Asheville, North Carolina. Actually, Mary Margaret Jenkins never once gave a thought to direction, as if the Dixon County Fair would suddenly appear before her if she drove long enough. She has a grand picture in her mind of the fair, of giant wheels and brightly colored ribbons, of the sounds of tinny music and jumbled voices, of the smells of frying burgers and roasting hot dogs, of bright sunlight and sawdust to walk upon. She imagined the tents concealing mysterious people and their secrets, and she envisioned herself entering a magic world where questions may be asked and answered. She seemed all her life to have an endless list of questions, and never a satisfying answer to any of them.

As she set out on her trip, it never once occurred to Mary Margaret that she didn't have a dime in her pocket, or that the gas gauge registered half-empty, or that she should ask permission to drive the car. Never mind. She wheeled the big car along the highway, scraping the gears, and banging on the brakes while she studied the scenery passing by the windows. Elroy's car picked up speed down the inclines while Mary Margaret's imagination wheeled along on a different highway. She thought she saw a peacock and took a deep cut in the road on a blind curve. A man with a load of Alberta peaches lost a box or two on the road after swerving his car to avoid hitting Mary Margaret.

She noted the woods ferns waving to her beside the edge of the road, like a family saying, "Hello," and a cluster of flowers like white bells growing out of a clump of rocks. She would stop and pick some on the way back. As she looked up from the ferns, a Greyhound bus met her at the lip of the hill, dead on. The bus swerved left, and Mary Margaret scraped the right side of Elroy's car along a metal guard rail. One foot to the right, the mountain dropped two hundred feet. She drove on, careening the car across the hill and going too far right, she ran the car through a long line of quilts on display beside the road. A man ran after her, but he could not catch up. A string of quilts dragged behind Elroy's car, and finally dropped one by one along the road. Mary Margaret was studying two white mules in a pasture.

Going down the other side of the mountain, Mary Margaret steered the center line of the road behind the car's hurling weight, all while she studied the colors of the mountains layered in light blues and deep purples. Mary Margaret never noticed that she had demolished a half dozen bee hives where she had misguided the car into a field, or that an unhappy woman had scowled when Mary Margaret ran Elroy's car through her marigolds. Mary Margaret hooked the front bumper on a junk car setting too near the road, and a bright piece of metal from the front of Elroy's car twirled into the weeds. She misguided the car around a deep curve and a tree limb smacked the windshield.

Where the road gives up its twists and turns at the bottom of the mountain, Elroy's car coasted to a stop on a straight narrow stretch of highway. Two large pastures lay on either side of the road where a farmer's cows grazed in an open space at the base of the mountains. Mary Margaret got out of the car and perched herself upon the warm hood of Elroy's Ford, her beak of a nose turned up toward the sun that hid itself like a wild head behind some trees. Mary Margaret sat on the hood eating a supper of peanut butter crackers and pickles, watching the dragon-mountains blaze in the sunset. Sometimes a car or a pickup truck blew a shrill horn and swerved around Elroy's Ford which had roosted like a giant green bird in the middle of the road and was difficult to see in the dimming light.

When the farmer living in a white house across the pasture came to run his cows into the milking barn, he spied Mary Margaret lying on the hood of Elroy's Ford. Seeing the spider-web crack in the windshield, he thought there had been an accident.

His temples pulsed with a rush of fear, and he ran through his cows and jumped the fence along the road. He came upon Mary Margaret in her dreamy repose, stretched flat out upon the warm hood of the car, her fingers woven under the nape of her neck, her elbows flared out like white wings from her shoulders. She stared straight up into the heavens. The farmer put questions to her. "Are you all right, girl?"

Mary Margaret kept a steady eye toward the night sky and replied, "Is there a wind among the stars? See the way the stars glitter like the underside of leaves when you lie down under a tree. There must be a mighty gushing wind blowing among the stars to make them glitter like leaves."

Elroy and Sam Dody came in Sam's truck bringing a five gallon can of gas to get the Ford running. They left their tobacco patch in the coolest part of the evening to collect Mary Margaret stranded miles from home on a dark road. The farmer, Bill Moody, had pushed the car off to the side of the road with Mary Margaret still dreaming on the hood.

"You ought to keep that girl penned up," he told Elroy, pushing his cap back on his head. "She's queer in the head."

Sam Dody had known Mary Margaret from her infancy. He roared in laughter at farmer Bill Moody's remarks. Sam Dody knew stories about Mary Margaret himself. He remembered a time when Mary Margaret jumped off the side of a hill into a big tub of cooled molasses, the time she let old man Hinkle's billy goats loose and they ate all his neighbors' gardens. Or, there was the time she climbed a tree to look at a woodpecker's nest, and Elroy spent half the day finding a ladder tall enough to get her back down. Sam Dody ran the scene of Mary Margaret perched like a chicken on the hood of Elroy's car through his head for the telling of a great story to the neighbors. A story about a loony girl who thinks there is a wind up there blowing in the heavens when everybody knows the heavens are as still as Sunday.

At the end of that summer when the tobacco was hung and the hay put in the barn, Elroy and Mary Margaret, piled into the Ford with an ample amount of fried chicken, slicing tomatoes, homemade biscuits, and apple pie. Elroy turned west out of the driveway toward Dixon. On Highway 181, he abruptly cut off at a truck stop.

"Mary Margaret," Elroy said, sliding out of the driver's seat, "why don't you drive us toward Dixon?"

Elroy sank back on the passenger side with his hands knitted behind the nape of his neck. He closed his eyes and pondered the tobacco patch late of a night, the sky clear as well water and crickets singing like a thousand rusty hinges. Mary Margaret drove the car, sitting on the edge of the seat, her hands firmly on the steering wheel and her feet stretched to the pedals. She drove toward Dixon with the great ease of someone who had driven a hundred years. She drove toward Dixon with a hundred years of Jenkins blood thinking in her hands and feet.

The Resurrection of Hannah Belle Hogan

Truman Hogan's mama, Hannah Belle Hogan, lay dying in her big feather tick bed. All the kinfolk had flocked home to Dixon County from faraway places. Truman's oldest sister, Martha, came all the way from Colorado. His other sisters, Jesse, Melva, and Sarah, had rushed in from such far corners of the map as Jackson, Memphis and Spartanburg. Their suitcases packed well, they had come for the long ordeal of death, and for putting things right afterwards. The sisters soon made themselves niches of territory about the small house after they had wasted their first day at the home place, fluttering aimlessly about, weeping, and a dabbing at the corners of their eyes with cotton print hankies. They hovered about the darkened death room like plump, white-breasted pigeons fluttering to roost on a place that is too small and crowded, cooing to each other in hushed voices.

Truman's brothers came, too. Woodrow came from Pontiac, Michigan, where he had gone to make cars for General Motors in 1951. And Roosevelt came in from Asheville, North Carolina, where he had worked for his wife's daddy's business since 1954. At night, they all took turns sitting up with their mama. For sleeping, the sisters had claimed all the sofas and beds, and the brothers made pallets of quilts and blankets on the sitting room floor.

During the day, the brothers kept out of the sisters' way. They cut and stacked a cord of wood. They carried buckets of water. Fed the cow. Mended the back steps that were near to collapsing. Mostly, they discussed what they would do with the farm when their poor mother passed on. They lowered their eyes beneath their ball caps and nodded their heads, solemnly, when a neighbor came by with a pie or a baked ham and made the sympathetic remark, "It won't be the same with Hannah Belle gone."

Sometimes they were off to visit neighbors and relatives who wanted word of their mother's condition. Sometimes they sat by their mother's deathbed, whispering in the darkened room about times passed, of days when the family worked the farm together, milked twenty-odd cows, put up hay, hoed corn in the sick-heat of the day and swam off the heat in the swimming hole late of the summer afternoons.

Truman had not seen his brothers and sisters all together for nearly three years gone Christmas when their father had passed away. Truman was the youngest, 14 years old and his mama's tag-a-long, born late in her life and the only child left at home.

Hannah Belle had been bedridden for two weeks before her children had flocked in. She had not moved a hair's breadth beneath her downy quilt for days, and the covers had molded to the shape of her body so that she looked like the marble lady lying peacefully atop Amanda Winfield's grave in the New Ebenezer Presbyterian Cemetery. Her arms had gone white and brittle like cold birch bark. They lay stiffly on top of the bedcovers like chunks of stove wood. Her eyes had not opened in days and her mouth was clinched closed in a fine line. The smooth curls of her white hair were waxed against her skull.

"Pneumonia," Doc Bailey had told them. He shook his head and listened with the round metal disk, moving it like checkers about her chest. "And she's not coughing," he said with his head sideways above Hannah Belle's chest. The family all took this for a telling sign that she was dying for sure.

"Maybe we could try an onion poultice on her chest," Truman said. "That might set her to coughing soon enough."

His sisters smiled softly at Truman's suggestion, a sad look of resignation in their eyes. "If penicillin won't work," said Martha, "then I don't see how an onion poultice will do much good. That's so old fashioned."

"On the other hand, it can't do any harm at this point," said Doc Bailey with a sympathetic look at young Truman. "There's not another thing that can be done for her," he said. "If we'd just caught it sooner." Doc Bailey shook his head and left with his coat across his left arm and his black bag in his right hand.

Truman set about peeling and slicing a gallon of white onions and frying them in a big iron skillet with bacon grease. The kitchen reeked of the pungent onions and hot bacon that he'd wrapped into a white dishtowel. Stinging tears welled up in everybody's eyes.

Truman pulled up a chair beside his mother's deathbed, and attended to the onion poultice so it would not burn her cold, delicate skin. He sat all that day with his mother, reheating the onion poultice, or frying up a new one when he thought the stinging smell was giving out. His eyes puffed up red and teary. His nose began to drip. The sisters refused to stay near the deathbed for any time at all because the pungent odor of the hot onions made them cough and weep.

By the end of the day, Melva and Jesse were coaxing Truman to quit the onion poultices. "How can we sit beside Mama with that suffocating smell in her room?"

But Truman attended the poultice or held his mama's hand atop the quilt and whispered, "Mama? Mama?" every time he saw her eyes circle beneath the transparent lids.

By the next morning, Hannah Bell Hogan was perking up some. She coughed violently, and spat up phlegm. Her eyes opened. A wheezing came from her throat. She said, "Wa-ter."

By the afternoon, she had wakened enough that the sisters felt they could rearrange the bedclothes and prop her up on two pillows.

Jesse, the middle sister, whispered to Melva and Sarah, "I've always heard that dying people rouse around before they pass on. It's like God's fooling you that they are getting better, and then sudden, they up and die."

And then Melva said, "Do you all remember when Aunt Clytie died? She sat bolt upright in her bed and declared that she never felt better. And a few days later we were all attending her funeral."

"Oh, I fear the worst for dear Mama," said Jesse, wringing her hanky around the fingers of her left hand.

Truman was not having any of that talk. He fixed himself firmly beside his mother's bed and promised that he would not leave her until her hands were busy doing her woman-work. Until she could stir apple butter, and can vegetables, and hoe corn in the garden. Until she could patch the knees of his overalls and fish a speck of dirt out of his eye with the corner of her apron, until she could flutter busily about the place as she usually did.

Hannah Belle moved her mouth slightly and opened her eyes half way. Truman bent his ear toward her. Her voice was so low and raspy he barely heard her words. "Truman, the farm work is so far behind. It weighs on my mind."

"It'll have to wait, Mama. We won't leave you until you get better," he said.

She coughed, and spoke in the weakest voice, "It would do me a world of good if you would clean the taters out of the cellar. They'll be sprouting eyes by now."

"I'm not leaving until you get better," he said in his firmest voice.

"Cut the tater eyes out and plant them." She spoke ever so slowly. "It would give my heart a rest to know the taters are planted."

Truman went obediently to the cellar carrying a burlap sack and a lantern. In the lantern light, he could see the earthen walls of the cellar and the wooden shelves where the Idaho potatoes had been spread. The potatoes had sprouted long, white bony fingers that pointed in all directions in the ghostly light.

"Taters always know when it's spring," Truman thought, "like it's planted in them to know when to sprout."

Truman cut the potatoes into sections, with a sprout to each section, and put them in the sack carefully. Then he went to the garden spot behind the house and hoed up a tater ridge, working the moldy earth until the huge mounds were loose like new-dug graves. Some farmers dug ridges only for sweet potatoes, but Truman knew he could get a better yield of potatoes if he planted them in loose soil.

Truman smiled to himself as he worked because he knew he could make a better tater ridge than anyone else in the family. His mama had told him so many times.

"Truman," he could hear her saying, "you'll be the envy of us all. When fall comes and men are cussing the hard ground, trying to dig taters out of red clay, you'll be forking big Idahoes up from the earth like it was no work a-tall."

Truman knew that his mama would not have asked his brothers

to do this job, and the thought made him proud. When he saw the sun on the lip of the hill, he knew he had worked the better part of the day.

"We've got two big tater ridges planted," he whispered to his mama, taking up her hand. The corners of her mouth pulled into a weak smile. She was propped up on two pillows, but she was still limp as a dishrag.

"I'm glad about the taters, Truman, but it would do me good to know the corn was ready for planting." Her blue eyes, weak and glazed over like dirty windowpanes, pleaded to Truman.

Truman knew why his mother worried. The varmints would be out foraging soon. "I'm afraid the mice and rats will eat up what's left of the planting corn," she whispered.

"I'll see to the corn in the morning, Mama, if it makes you rest easier."

Next morning, Truman went to the corncrib, shucked what was left of the field corn, and piled the best ears in the corner of the crib. He lined up enough buckets to equal a bushel. He rubbed off row after row of the hard kernels, which pinged against the bucket as he dashed them in by the handful. His calloused hands burned against the rock-hard grains.

All the while, Truman could hear his daddy teaching him about shelling corn. "Shell off the nubbins from the point end and throw them in another bucket to feed the hogs. They're not fit for planting. Shell off only the regular, even grains down the middles of the cob. Leave the crooked grains on the bottom of the ear and throw them to the hogs, too. They won't make corn."

By suppertime, Truman had shelled a bushel of corn. "That's enough corn to plant a good six acres of land. Enough to feed two pigs and the milk cow all winter. Enough to take to the mill for grinding cornmeal, and enough to spare for next year's planting," he thought.

Truman knew even before he told his mama that the corn was shelled, that she would be worrying about the plowing. "There's no planting without plowing first," she would say.

"Mama? Look. I brought you some snow lilies. They bloomed up by the corncrib." He put the little bunch of flowers in a snuff glass and set them on a table by the bed. "Spring is coming early. The willows by the pond are budding out already."

"Has it rained ?" said Hannah Belle.

"No, Mama. Dry as a bone."

"Better plow the corn field and the sass patch before the rain comes." There was a hollow ring in his mama's voice.

Truman thought his mama's skin felt cooler, though. Martha had spoon-fed her mother a cup of beef broth. A good sign. But, Hannah Belle's weak head still rolled about the pillow like a newborn baby's.

"I'll see about getting the tractor started tomorrow."

"Truman. Don't be worrying Mama with all this farm talk," said Woodrow, pulling up a chair on the other side of the bed. "There's enough work to do here to kill a body off. The fence posts around the pasture are rotted out and the wire is rusted and broke in places. There's only one cow left on the place worth milking, and not enough silage left to feed her until spring pastures green up. What you need to do, Mama, is sell this old place off and come live with me or Roosevelt."

"You've got a head full of notions," said Truman. His daddy would turn over in his grave if he could hear Woodrow talking like that.

Hannah Belle Hogan looked wild-eyed from out of the white pillow. She tried to raise her head.

"See how you've got Mama bothered up?" Truman said. "Don't you worry, Mama. I'll see to the plowing. And Woodrow here can help me get the old tractor started." Truman made a face at his brother. "He works for General Motors, you know. He can help me fix whatever's wrong with the tractor."

Woodrow and Truman went to the barn and threw a ragged tarpaulin off the old John Deere. Woodrow looked into the engine, pulled at the carburetor wires, fingered about the alternator, and fidgeted with the battery cables.

"Can you tell what's the matter?" said Truman. "It won't turn over a lick."

"Well, I don't know much about engines," said Woodrow.

"Ain't you learned a sight about motors up there in Pontiac?"

"I don't put engines together. I put them in the car already put together." Woodrow explained by drawing a picture in the air with his hands. "See, the engine hangs down from this big conveyor belt, and me and two other men lower it into the car and bolt it on. And sometimes we hang doors, and sometimes we put on the hoods or the wheels or whatever the foreman tells us to do," said Woodrow.

"You mean you ain't learned a thing about how engines run? Why, I thought you worked on engines."

"It's damned hard work." The blood rose in Woodrow's cheeks. "It's hard work hornswoggling a damned eight hundred pound engine down into the sockets of them cars. I've mashed my hands off many a time. It's damned hard, back-breaking work hanging a car door so it's not put on crooked and has to be done over." Woodrow's voice echoed around the rafters of the barn. "I'm right proud of it myself."

The next morning, Truman went to see Ebenezer Jones who owned the farm next to theirs. Ebenezer could not lend him a tractor, but he could spare his three plow mules, Joe, Dave, and Jack. Truman borrowed Eb's flat-bottomed plow for turning sod.

Truman hitched Jack on the right for lead, Dave in the middle for steadying, and Joe on the outside left to pivot the hard turns. Truman struggled to keep the plow points down in the earth at first. The mules set them skating across the ground when Truman didn't keep a tight grip and a firm pressure on the plow handles. Truman had to back the mules up many times and start the rows over.

Some of the rows were great long S's and some were Z's. But by the end of the day, the mules had turned up a fair amount of fine, black earth. Truman put a handful of the soft dirt into his overalls pocket.

"Mama. I'm making right good progress with the plowing. Eb Jones lent me the use of his mules and flat bottom, and we'll have a right smart plowing done in a few days if the weather holds," Truman said. His mother seemed right pert when he described the plowing.

"The ground plowed the finest I've ever seen it. See here?" Truman dug the handful of soft earth out of his pocket and put it into his mother's hand.

"I can feel the spring coming in this dirt," she said. A pink blush came up her cheeks ever so slightly. She worked at making the dirt into a ball inside the curve of her weak fingers.

"You can smell the spring in this dirt, too," Truman said. "It smells like a cold mush melon."

Truman understood his mother. He understood there was something in the earth that called out to be planted and hoed and watered. He knew the longing to feel silky dirt between his fingers, to see green things bud, to feel his spirit rise like sap when planting times comes.

"Truman?" Woodrow said at the supper table. "Me and Roosevelt have been talking to Eb Jones about buying the farm. He's agreeable to $300 per acre, top dollar these days. Back in '56 you couldn't get $200 per acre. The farm's run down awful, but the land is level and there's a good pond for cattle and a creek on the lower side."

"Me and Mama won't listen to none of that talk," said Truman.

"Roosevelt says Mama can come live with them for awhile, if she gets better, and then me and Madge can have her for awhile." Roosevelt nodded.

"And Sarah says you're welcome to come live with her. She's got a boy about your age, and you two can have a grand old time. Besides, it's proper time you got back to school. Ain't that right, Sarah?"

Sarah, who was taking a pan of biscuits out of the oven, turned and nodded in agreement.

"I told you me and Mama won't hear any of that talk," said Truman.

"Why, this old farm has about killed Mama off," piped in Roosevelt at the end of the table. "These bitter cold winters. And her chopping wood and fetching in. And her trying to scratch enough garden sass out of that puny patch for canning, to barely live through the winters. I'm surprised she ain't died before now."

"Mama ain't dying. And she ain't leaving this farm," shouted Truman.

Next day, Truman walked about the farm surveying what needed to be done to set things straight. He knew that he must do a man's work on the farm or be parceled out with his mother like hand-me-downs.

Truman finished the plowing, and took the mules home. Then he set about cutting and barking cedar trees for fence posts. He restrung the spiky, rusted barbwire along the pasture as best he could, twisting the broken ends together in places. His mother beamed when he told her about it.

"I'm going to clean out the barn and manure the corn field before planting. The sign is in the thighs and it will work in good."

Truman was just coming to the house after laying off the garden plot when he met Woodrow, red-faced and hot-footing it off the front porch, his black traveling satchel in one hand and his hat in the other. He stopped dead in the middle of the front yard when he met Truman coming toward the house. "I was trying to talk sense to that old woman in there," he said, "and you know what she done? She threw a damned dirt clod right in my face! I reckon you put her up to that."

Truman had no chance to explain about the dirt, for Woodrow marched off toward his car in a huff. His new 1958 Chevy Impala screeched down the dirt road, leaving a trail of red dust swirling in his wake.

Doc Bailey came that afternoon to see Hannah Belle Hogan. "I thought I'd come to see the dying, but I do believe that Hannah Belle Hogan has come back to us from the drop side of yonder." She was sitting up in bed with her hands folded in her lap.

Roosevelt packed up his suitcase and went back to his family in Asheville. Melva, Jesse, and Sarah scattered toward their own homes in a few days' time. Martha, the eldest child, was appointed to stay on until things could be set straight again. "After all," said Sarah, "Doc Bailey says if she can throw dirt out of her own grave, then he thinks she'll live a season or two longer."

"I'm of a mind to plant sweet peas again this year," said Hannah Belle, recuperating in her feather tick bed. "And some Silver Queen sweet roasting ears." She pointed out the window toward the plowed garden. Truman had come in from the fields. He sat in a chair nearby with his elbows propped on his knees.

"Pick up some runner beans at the Co-Op. We can plant them

with the corn. Say them turnips will be up soon? I've had a taste in my mouth for greens and pot liquor. Be sure to plant some leaf lettuce on the shady side of the smoke house, else it'll sun-scorch." Hannah Belle Hogan ran her sentences together in her usual way.

"Truman?" she said as an afterthought, "Did you remember to buy some onion slips?"

Where the Fishes Swim

The heat was oppressive that July in Tennessee. A farmer might have called it good corn growing weather, but it was oppressive and suffocating with humidity. It had just gone noon and the white hot sun stung the tops of my arms as I stood by the front yard gate waiting for Mr. John's old black farmhand, Silas Mosely, to come walking by. I had spotted him coming across the top of the hill, scuffling a red dust cloud behind him, and I knew he would be passing our house soon.

Old Silas was easy to recognize, even from a distance. He was tall and lean, quick-moving most times, but that day he came slowly and deliberately, dragging the soles of his shoes through the dusty road.

As Silas drew closer, I could see great circles of sweat running under his armpits and across the chest of his khaki shirt. Silas always wore khaki, always clean and pressed, sometimes patched, always a felt hat, round-brimmed and grease stained about the headband. Years of hard work had stooped his shoulders. That day I could not see his black face beneath his hat brim for the added weight of a burlap sack slung over his back had bent him over at the waist.

Silas has a sack of corn to husk, I thought, or a bit of feed to take to Myrtle, our brood mare, who was grazing in the sun-burnt pasture beyond the woods. We would take Myrtle to the river for a cool drink. We would paddle along the edge of the river in a quiet shady place and wash the dust off our feet, just as we always did.

Perhaps Silas had a sack of apples from Mr. John's cellar. We would make cider from the leftover June apples and drink it in the heat of the evening. Silas was coming to borrow the cider press. My grandfather had made the press himself, an old wooden one with a round barrel, a round wooden plate, and a long metal screw between the handle and the plate. Mr. John would be along directly to supervise the cider making. A tart spring cider, one with bite, that's what Mr. John liked.

But Silas stopped at our gate and opened the sack to show me five puppies, brown and white spotted balls of fur wiggling over one another, crying as the sunlight rushed in on them. I reached into the sack and ran my fingers down the softness of their backs, felt their rough tongues licking along the tips of my fingers.

Then Silas drew out a new quarter from his pocket and, showing it to me, he said, "I knowed what Mr. John wanted soon as he handed me this here quarter, and I knowed they was nothing I could do 'cept do as I'm told!"

"Now, Silas, what did Mr. John tell you to do?" I asked him.

"Mr. John say get rid of these here pups. He say they's all bitch dogs and they's all mongrels to boot and he say get rid of these here pups anyways I could. He say I could take a hammer, but I never could do a thing like that. So he say drown them pups in the river. Just don't come bringing them back. That's what he say."

Silas took off his hat and rubbed his bald head, which was as smooth and brown as a river slick, and then he picked up the sack and slid it up across his back and walked in the direction of the river.

I had told Mama that Silas was coming by and could I please go. She said it was okay as long as I minded, and so I fell in behind him.

The dirt road was baked in the sunshine and the hot gravel stung my bare feet. I had forgotten my sandals again. I remember watching the road for the hot gravel and saying to Silas, "You don't have to do everything Mr. John tells you to, Silas."

"Yes sir, I do. I knowed when that bitch had pups what would have to be done, and what old nigger man would have to do it. I knowed it shore."

Then I said to the back of him that maybe Mama would let me keep the pups. Silas said he knew better than to do a trick like leaving five bitch dogs on a good neighbor.

Down the road a short way we cut off across a meadow toward the river and followed a cow path over the slope of green pasture, down through the bottomland where a crop of tobacco grew waist high to Silas. The leaves hit me at eye level, and the strong smell of green tobacco suffocated me. Gummy leaves stuck at my arms and legs as we waded through the patch. The bottomland had been plowed between the rows with the roto-tiller and the fine, silky dirt squished up in puffs between my toes like brown talcum powder.

We got to the river quickly, for it wasn't far from my house. We could hear the hum of water before we could see the river. A row of large locust and sycamore trees guarded the riverbank; the underbellies of their leaves shimmered white-silver in the sunshine. We passed beneath the high ceiling of branches and found the pathway that unwound like a flat brown ribbon and ran alongside the riverbank for miles and miles downstream.

The Nolichucky was crystal that day. Silas said that the clearness was unnatural, low and slow as a creek dribbling along. Things that usually remained in the muddiness were revealed like long hidden secrets. We could see brown river slicks on the bottom, and the slimy sticks and rotted leaves tangled among them. Mussel shells lay in a heap under the water where a raccoon had been feasting. Crawdads picked about the river bottom, backing in and out of the river rocks. Two small bluegills were trapped, gasping air in a puddle along the bank. Silas waded in and threw them flipping and fighting into the safety of the river.

"I tell you we'll be needing rain right soon. This river's too clean. We need a good muddying rain to bring this river up," Silas said as he took up his sack and picked his way down the path slowly in front of me.

Saw briars overgrowing the edge of the pathway grabbed at my bare legs and drew a long string of red droplets. I was wearing a dress that day. Mama would fuss about my scratched legs; a young lady, she'd say, shouldn't go about with long, red briar scratches up and down her legs. And there was church tomorrow, too.

We walked silently. Except for a solitary crow squawking in the distance, and the brush of our bodies in tall grass there were no sounds. In the stillness I asked Silas, "Why did you take that quarter anyway? Maybe you shouldn't have taken the quarter, Silas?"

"That quarter ain't got nothing to do with it, Youngon," he said, stopping and leaning way out over the riverbank looking downstream. "When you grown up big, you can see why the quarter ain't got nothing to do with it."

And then he said, "It's giving the quarter got just as much to do with it as taking the quarter. Because sometimes a nigger's got to take it, but you don't have to give it to him, now does you?"

Silas shifted the sack to the other side of his back and moved slowly onto the pathway. I trooped behind him; close enough to see a hundred beggar's lice sticking to the backs of his khaki legs, moving rhythmically in the folds of his pants as he walked. The sack swung above my head. As the puppies wiggled and bumped in the sack, I would smell their breath panting warm and moist through the burlap.

Silas stopped abruptly and I bumped into the back of him. He turned off the pathway and sat down in a clearing near the riverbank beneath a large Catawba tree whose limbs spread like monstrous shaggy arms above the river. I sat beside the wiggling sack.

"We could just turn them loose here, Silas, and nobody would ever know."

"No, Youngon. The foxes would eat them up right away," he said. "It's a mercy to send them on where the fishes go. These dogs ain't no use to nobody. It's a mercy to send them swimming."

Silas fanned himself with his hat and contemplated the river. He was far away, his mind drifting down river with the humming water, his knees pulled up under his chin, his arms across them. He picked a tall blade of saw grass and chewed on the end of it. And so I picked some grass, too, and chewed the sweetness out of it.

The river was green near the bank where the shade lay on the water, the smell of muddiness gone, the fish blowing circles, spreading to nothingness. Silas kept his eye on the river and said, "It's a sad thing to be a mongrel on this here earth, now ain't it. Fit for nothing but the river water. Fit to go where the fishes go."

Silas and I came to a place on the Nolichucky we called the Puddle Hole where we often fished in quiet, deep water. An ancient uprooted beech tree leaned right-angled above the river. Silas turned the quarter over and over between his thumb and forefinger, and then he sent it slicing through the water. I remember thinking he would change his mind now that he was rid of the quarter, but he said to me angrily, "I done told you, time and again, it ain't the quarter, Youngon!"

Silas dug his heels into the riverbank and brought the sack up to shoulder level. He swung it back and forth, low to the ground and then up as high as his shoulder, and then he let it go. The sack turned somersaults above the water and splashed down clear beyond the end of the beech log, making great waves in the river. But there must have been air in the sack because it began to bob and sink, and bob and sink.

I held my breath until it hurt my chest, and I stared at the sack until my eyes blurred over. I could not blink away the blindness, like sun in my eyes. Something was pressing the breath out of me, but I could not see what it was.

And then I could see Silas with a sack of Mr. John's June apples. I could see him setting up grandfather's apple cider press. Mr. John was saying to Silas that the apples were good this year for cider.

Mr. John wanted to mash the apples first, before he put them in the press. They were hard and tart, and he handed the sack to Silas and said, "Mash the apples with the heel of your boot, Silas. Mash them right in the sack." Silas stomped the sack until the apple pulp oozed up through the burlap. Then Mr. John said, "Pour them into the press, Silas, and put the wooden plate tightly over the mashed apples." Then Mr. John tried hard to turn the press handle, but he could not make the juice come out into the little pail under the spout.

"Silas. You press the apples," Mr. John said. Silas turned the handle until the good, clear apple juice gurgled out into the pail. He bore down harder and harder on the screw handle, and Mr. John smiled at the juice and said it would make a good tart cider. He stuck his finger in the pail and sucked off the juice. Mr. John said, "Silas. Press them apples right down to the skins." So Silas stopped and rolled up his khaki sleeves above his elbows. And when he pressed down hard again, his face blew up tight, and black ropes came up along his neck.

Mr. John, smiling down at the apple juice, said, "Just a few more turns, Silas, and you'll have those apples pressed out good. And Silas turned down hard on the handle until his arms trembled under the strain, and he blew spit out of the corners of his mouth.

Finally, it was done. He gave the handle a twirl and the plate spun up, and the breath came rushing back into my chest, like someone blowing me up like a balloon.

I blinked the river clear again. There was nothing but the humming water. I whispered up to Silas who was leaning out limber as a fishing pole over the river, "Are they gone now, Silas?"

Silas did not answer directly; he kept his eye on the river. At last Silas said in a low voice, "I ought to know by now about putting a rock or two in the sack. You'd think I'd know by now about the rocks."

Tizzie Dearstone's Night Lace

Every morning at 7:30 on the dot, if it isn't raining, Tizzie Dearstone walks to her clothesline to hang up her freshly laundered lingerie. Her big hips rotate like two huge sacks of flour under her floral print house dress. Tizzie rubs the clothesline with a towel in her fat hand until it is squeaky clean, and then she carefully fastens the two spaghetti straps of *Night Lace*, a skimpy onepiece design she mailordered from Regina's Seductive Secrets Catalog.

Tizzie Dearstone is enormously fat, and her skin is shiny pink like a plastic doll's. Her short, blond curls lie in tight ringlets on her head as if they are set in plaster, and her cheeks are puffy and glow like polished apples around her square turned up nose.

There isn't much to Tizzie Dearstone's nightie, thin spaghetti straps, a g-string, and not much black lace between. And her neighbors, that is her female neighbors, wonder how she gets into that nightie.

Mamie, Grace, and Sandra are puzzled by Tizzie's morning ritual. Mamie has decided that her actions border on aberrant behavior. Mamie uses the word, aberrant, since she has taken an Introduction to Psychology course at the Dixon Community College and remembers the word from a midterm examination: Deviation from the normal or usual; DERANGEMENT, in all capitals, the book defines it. She remembers the word clearly since she missed the definition on her exam. Mamie likes to apply her psychology lessons to real situations, so she studies Tizzie's ritual and takes meticulous notes on a pocketsized writing pad.

Mamie Johnson, who lives in the Wylie Dixon Subdivision opposite Tizzie's house, says the lingerie looks like something that got chewed up by the washing machine.

Grace Treadwell, who lives next door to Tizzie, on the bedroom side of the Dearstone house, says it looks like the old nylon underwear her husband Buford uses to wipe his hands on after he changes the oil in his car.

Sandra Gambol, who lives next door to the Dearstones, on the kitchen side of their house, went so far as to order the catalog so she could study the lingerie up close. Her daughter, Haley, who is a junior in high school, gave her the catalog idea when she said about Tizzie's lingerie, "Jeez, a cool rag from Regina's Seductive Secrets!" Sandra got up her nerve and went to Ziggie's Bookstore where a nice salesgirl found the address on a computer. Sandra is amazed by computers, but she is also afraid of them. She noticed that the salesgirl could punch the keys without looking at the keyboard.

"*Night Lace*," Sandra tells her neighbors who have gathered at her house to look at the catalog, "is meant to depict the dreaminess of a starstudded sky." Sandra shows them the catalog spread carefully across her knees. She sits stiffly in her chair and avoids touching the pictures.

Grace Treadwell looks at the catalog over Sandra's shoulder. "I can't see for the world why any woman would waste good money on that trashy garb." A nude model wearing only pink feathers over her pubic area has caught Grace's attention.

Mamie Johnson takes the catalog out of Sandra's lap and flips the pages with her acrylic fingernails. "*Night Lace* is not an appropriate name since obviously there are more stars than night sky. But, generally speaking, girls, I think this is a real tease and we should all order. I think I'd look great in *Pink Flamingo*."

"You're a blackguard!" Grace sticks her tongue out at Mamie, half joking and half rebuking. "Buford would call me a hussey if he saw me in such a getup." Grace pulls her dress tail down over her knees. "You better burn that catalog before the men around here get the wrong idea."

Sandra Gambol burns the catalog on Tuesday's rubbish pile after she studies the pictures and commits several designs to memory. As she watches the bare legs and brilliant laces curl and blacken in the fire, she wonders what Mamie and Grace would think if they knew she has also burned on her memory the pictures of svelte young women with smooth thighs and high bosoms clad only in skimpy patches of satin and seethrough stretch lace.

Tizzie is married to Rupert Dearstone, a tall, wiry man who drives a delivery truck for the Magic-Dough Bakery. The Dearstones have been married for twenty three years, but have no children.

Tizzie's neighbors attribute her being fat to Rupert's bringing home the day-old cakes, pies, and bakery goods each evening in a large box. "Rupert likes to keep Tizzie fat so that other men will not look at her. Some men are strange like that," Sandra says. The neighbors call the Dearstones Mr. and Mrs. Jack Spratt.

Rupert drives to work in his Magic-Dough delivery truck at 7 a.m. each morning. The Dearstones' kitchen lights come on at 5 a.m. Their large picture windows and sheer curtains make it easy to see inside the Dearstones' kitchen. Lately, Sandra, Mamie, and Grace have seen strange movements through the blurry morning light of Tizzie's nylon curtains.

It is early one morning that Sandra Gambol zigzags across the street to Mamie Johnson's house and pounds frantically on her back door. "I'd swear that Rupert is beating Tizzie!" she speaks hysterically.

Sandra and Mamie run back to Sandra's house where they can look clearly into the Dearstones' kitchen window. Grace, drinking her first cup of coffee by the kitchen window, sees her neighbors racing back and forth in a flurry of bath robes and bobbing curlers, and she slips on her scuffs and runs down the street to Sandra's house to find out what is going on.

"I do not believe in a million years that Rupert would beat Tizzie!" Sandra closes her eyes and shakes her hands emphatically.

"She's too big to beat up," agrees Mamie, peering into the Dearstones' kitchen through a crack in Sandra's curtains. "If Rupert tried to hit Tizzie, he'd be larded." Mamie says that a clearer explanation is that the Dearstones are taking dancing lessons and they practice their steps early in the morning.

Tizzie and Rupert seem to be whirling around the kitchen from where the coffee pot is on the counter to the dinette table. Sometimes they dip through the living room doorway, and then they disappear.

Mamie is convinced that the Dearstones are doing a Tango. "What else would explain the violent bending, lashing, kicking and thrashing movements," she says. Mamie bends backward and kicks her heels toward the ceiling.

"Come here and look at this," says Sandra. Tizzie and Rupert roll on top of the kitchen table. Tizzie's body seems to be engulfing Rupert. "But there is no music playing!" Grace shouts back at Mamie, who is still dancing around the kitchen with a breakfast plate.

"No, he's really trying to beat her up," screams Sandra. She watches the Dearstones' kitchen like a TV soap opera. "Tizzie is fighting back!"

Grace sits down heavily on a kitchen chair and reports the odd behavior she's observed at the Dearstones. "Tizzie never hangs out her wash on Monday and Wednesday mornings anymore. Normally, Tizzie washes sheets, towels, and underwear on Mondays, and pants, shirts, and dresses on Wednesdays. I know, because I'm on the clothesline side of the house. Now, all that Tizzie ever hangs on her clothesline is that tacky lingerie. That *Night Lace* thing from the catalog. And, if you think that is odd, you should notice what happens over there every evening."

"What happens over there every evening?" Sandra and Mamie ask in chorus.

"Nothing," says Grace. "Nothing at all. Rupert comes home at 5:30 each evening. The place is all dark. Rupert goes in, but they never come out. They never say boo to a goose. Rupert never mows the lawn. Look what a mess it's getting to be."

Sandra is the one to say that someone should speak to Tizzie about the strange behavior. "If Rupert is beating her, we ought to stop him."

Sandra Gambol, Mamie Johnson, and Grace Treadwell sit before Pastor Goforth of Cedar Grove United Methodist Church, a country church attended by many families in the neighborhood, including the Dearstones. Pastor Goforth is a small, quiet man in his mid-fifties. He sits poised behind his desk in the church manse with his hands clasped under his chin. He considers himself to be a good listener, and fastens his eyes carefully upon his visitors as they speak.

Sandra thinks to herself that Pastor Goforth's eyes magnified to the size of quarters by the thick convex lenses of his wire-rimmed glasses make him seem all-knowing.

Mamie quickly opens her psychology book and reads the passages on aberrant behavior. Mamie then carefully describes the Dearstones' odd thrashing each morning, and Grace describes *Night Lace* in great detail. "We would show you a picture of *Night Lace,* Pastor Goforth, but Sandra burned the one she had." Mamie jabs Grace in the ribs with the corner of her pocketbook.

"Rupert has seemed peculiar lately," Grace continues, shifting her chair away from Mamie's. "He hasn't mowed the lawn in the last six weeks. The grass is knee deep over there. Buford is going to speak to Rupert about it if something isn't done soon. A messy yard like that drags the whole neighborhood down."

Mamie aims a sharp glance at Grace. "That really seems irrelevant to this discussion."

"Don't use that tone with me, Miss Uppity. You've been a know-it-all ever since you stared taking courses at the Dixon Community College."

Pastor Goforth changes the subject. "Maybe Rupert hasn't been feeling well lately. There may be a simple explanation."

He thinks of the visit Tizzie paid him a few weeks ago. She had been crying and her puffy eyes were ringed with dark circles. The small chair across from his desk had seemed to disappear under Tizzie, so that she seemed to be sitting magically in mid-air. She was wearing a lime green polyester pants suit and a brightly flowered blouse. Large rolls of Tizzie's soft flesh had puffed out under the tight seams of her clothing.

Suddenly she'd opened her purse, brought out a pair of red lace panties shaped like a heart, and scooted them across the desk. Pastor Goforth had taken out his handkerchief and blown his nose, a method he'd learned from a professor in seminary to stall for time in uncertain situations.

"Rupert is having an affair," Tizzie has said, almost stoically.

Tizzie told him how she'd discovered the red lace panties in Rupert's delivery truck one Saturday afternoon. She was standing in the back of the truck, helping Rupert tidy up bread boxes and cake wrappers. Rupert's truck is always cleaned every weekend, a company policy to keep bugs out of the bakery goods. Rupert goes to get the garden hose and a broom. When Tizzie picks up a Magic-Dough bread box, stuck underneath are red lace G-string panties. Size 5, Regina's Seductive Secrets, the label is marked.

The red lace panties smell like bread. Tizzie stretches the lace heart up to the light toward the back of the truck. Her face feels on fire in the heat of the truck.

Tizzie had related to Pastor Goforth the motion picture playing in her mind. Rupert and a mysterious, slim siren making passionate love on the floor of the dark delivery truck. The mysterious siren wearing nothing but the red lace panties. Her white, luminous body glistening as if it has been sprinkled all over with confectioners' sugar, contrasting with the shining red-heart of panties. Rupert and the siren, in a state of wild delirium, are mashing flat the boxed loaves of Magic-Dough bread, grappling each other over boxes of angel food cakes and apple pies. Rupert is wearing his blue Magic-Dough delivery uniform, the mysterious siren is tearing at his buttons with long red fingernails.

After Tizzie had told her story, Pastor Goforth had advised that she try to communicate with Rupert, listen to his side of the story before doing anything rash.

Pastor Goforth hears Grace Treadwell saying, "I think something bad is going on at the Dearstone house." Grace takes a cotton hankie out of her purse and wipes her eyes. She sits straight on the edge of her chair, and holds her pocketbook like a shield.

"My good lord," says Sandra, holding her kitchen curtains aside for Mamie and Grace. Pastor Goforth is coming to see Tizzie today.

"I hope she doesn't take IT in too soon." Grace scours the sky for signs of rain. "Watermelon red," says Grace. Grace and Mamie huddle at Sandra's kitchen window and study Tizzie's clothesline. Instead of *Night Lace*, new red lingerie featuring large cut-outs for the breasts and a flirty little short skirt is hanging on Tizzie's clothesline. Mamie, holding a cup, stirs sugar into her coffee. "I'd say fuchsia."

Sandra is too embarrassed to say that she knows Tizzie's new lingerie is called *Scarlet Encounter*, located on page 53 of Regina's Seductive Secrets Catalog. Since she ordered the first catalog, Sandra has been receiving others regularly. It never occurred to her that her name would be placed on a mailing list. Also, in yesterday's mail, Sandra got a special offer for an exciting black leather ensemble with cut-outs in the buns and bust. She quickly stuffed the catalog into the trash.

Grace has made a freshly baked Brown Sugar and Raisin Swirl coffee cake, a recipe she cut out of Wednesday's newspaper. The

Guiding Light is playing on a small TV in Sandra's kitchen. Sandra's wishes she had learned to program the VCR so she could tape her show and watch it later, but she is afraid to push the buttons. Something might break. Grace and Mamie are not watching TV. Instead, they have taken their coffee cups to the kitchen table and are talking about General Norman Schwarzkopf.

"I never really noticed before," says Mamie, "but I have decided BIG men are really appealing. You know, in a physical way." Mamie mashes out a cigarette in a cracked blue-willow saucer, a make-do ashtray. Grace does not allow Buford to smoke.

Grace stiffens against the back of her chair. "Law, you do say the wildest things sometimes."

"I heard you say yourself once that John Goodman is your favorite actor, and you wouldn't mind playing Roseanne Arnold's part." Mamie smiles and blows smoke seductively.

"I think John Goodman is an excellent actor. You know that's all I meant." Grace bristles and takes a bite of her coffee cake.

Mamie has always been the liberated one, Sandra thinks. Mamie even had an affair with a married man, before she got married herself. Now she is a church-going woman, but to Sandra, Mamie seems to be feisty.

Mamie's husband, Jim, seems to like her that way. Last year for their thirtieth wedding anniversary, Jim gave Mamie a ticket to the *Chippendales* show playing at a Knoxville nightclub. Jim even drove her down himself. Mamie told Sandra and Grace about the show. "Hard, young bodies going to waste out there on that dance floor. Like being on the ocean and not being able to drink the water," she laughed. "And you should get a load of them rich, old ladies screaming and stuffing $5 and $10 bills down their underwear. I'm dumb. I took $1 bills. It's hard to compete with the big money. Of course, they jump back before you can get a feel. You should all come with me next time," Mamie told them.

"You're forgetting that we are decent women," says Grace.

Sandra thinks it would be fun to see the *Chippendales*. She has always tried to think clean thoughts, but lately she feels strangely tantalized by the seductive lingerie in the Regina's Seductive Secrets Catalog. She visualizes herself lying languidly across her bed, her black lace lingerie stretched tautly across her body, the black spaghetti straps dangling off her shoulders, her husband Odell's big frame outlined like a shadow in the bedroom door.

For the first time, Sandra is oddly aware of herself and Grace, of their plump and plodding ways. She and Grace are about as appealing as two fatly feathered setting hens rooting out comfortable dust holes in a barnyard.

Grace is only 43 years old, but her hair has gone gray. "I wouldn't peroxide my head for the world," she brags when Mamie tells her she ought to have her hair done. Grace wears her stockings rolled above her knees. "I think I am going through the change of life," She fans herself with a rolled up newspaper. "Hot flashes." Grace runs her napkin over her neck and under her dress collar.

Sandra takes note of her own plain, cotton dress with stretchable elastic waistband. Sandra buys flat, durable laceup shoes, the dark ones like cleaning women wear. Lately, she has stopped going to the beauty shop on Fridays to have her hair done, and she buys makeup off the sale table at Revco.

Always Sandra has prided herself on being plain. Now, she sees herself in contrast to Mamie who is wearing black stretch pants and skinny sandals that tie in long leather strings around her ankles. Mamie's toenails are painted bright red. Sandra's brogans look like old woman's shoes.

"I know I'm not the greatest beauty in the world," says Grace, her finger playing with a cake crumb on the table, "but wouldn't it be a shame to be as fat as Tizzie Dearstone. It's a wonder Rupert would live with her." Grace's words pull upon Sandra like the iron taste of cistern water.

"Rupert is taking me to Myrtle Beach for our twenty-fourth wedding anniversary next month," Tizzie tells Pastor Goforth who thinks her face shines like a newlywed's. Tizzie is wearing a pale blue muumuu with soft pink flowers on a ruffle along the hem. Tizzie floats like a blue cloud across the room as she goes for the coffee pot. Tizzie likes ruffles. There are ruffles on the curtains and on the sofa cushions. On top of the television set and the matching end tables are ruffled doilies.

"I think your dress is becoming," Pastor Goforth says.

"Oh, thank you, Pastor Goforth." Tizzie sits down on an armless chair near the end of the sofa and smoothes her dress.

"Mavis Stonebrook, my *Color-Me-Perfect* consultant, picked this out for me. You know, Pastor Goforth, I was really a mess until Mavis straightened me out. Why, I always thought I wore a size 52, but I'm really a size 56, and my wardrobe was all the wrong colors, dark and dingy. Mavis showed me that I'm a Spring designation on her color chart. I never realized I'm really light and bright.

A doily-lined plastic tray arranged with two dozen Magic--Dough donuts sprinkled with confectioner's sugar sits atop the coffee table. Tizzie offers Pastor Goforth a donut and takes one herself. She eats the donut in one bite. Tizzie pours two mugs of coffee. Pastor Goforth takes the blue mug that says *Visit Ruby Falls.*

Tizzie blows steam off the hot coffee. "I make coffee with chicory. I hope you like it. Rupert was stationed in Louisiana when he was in the army, and he got to liking his coffee with chicory." Tizzie sucks in a hot mouthful of coffee and eats another donut.

"You see, Pastor Goforth. Now I do everything Rupert likes, and he adores me. My prayers are answered because I took your advice. You remember that day I came to see you and you said I should pray for myself. Well, when I got home I leaned against the bed, and I prayed until I thought my head would bust open, and that made me feel a lot better. Then I called my Mama. At first I didn't want to bother Mama because she worries too much. She is old now and has pain in her lower back. But she said to me not to be disheartened. *The Lord works in mysterious ways his wonders to perform.* Well, I decided to let the Lord take care of this matter and just go on about my business. It wasn't five minutes after I hung up the phone that some voice came to me and said, *Go open that top dresser drawer in the spare bedroom.* And I went directly and opened that drawer, and what did I see, Pastor Goforth, but the thing that saved me and Rupert."

Suddenly, Tizzie launches herself up from her chair with both arms and floats toward another room. Tizzie floats back into the room, and she hands Pastor Goforth a book. Pastor Goforth reads the cover: *How to make your marriage come alive!" #1 Bestseller. The Total Woman.*

By Marabel Morgan.

Tizzie pops another donut into her mouth. "I've had that book tucked away in my dresser for twenty years. As I recall, I won it at the Saturday night Bingo. I was disappointed I won a book. I wanted that brown lamp that Geneva Hensley bingoed, and I tried to trade with her, but she looked at the book and said, "Looks like trash to me." Then I tried giving it away to Betty May Inscore and then to Bertha Jones, but their noses went snurley. So I took Marabel Morgan home, and put her in that top drawer in the spare room."

Pastor Goforth thumbs through *The Total Woman.* "She's a Christian," says Tizzie. She tells Pastor Goforth to see the last page for a complete list of scriptural references on marriage and sexual love.

"Read Chapter 10." Tizzie points her donut at the book. "It says that sexy lingerie is okay. I order mine from Regina's Seductive Secrets Catalog, but it doesn't really fit me right, so I let Rupert wear it." Tizzie pops another donut into her mouth.

Pastor Goforth hears Tizzie say through the ringing in his ears, "I've got that Saran Wrap teaser down real good. Every afternoon, I meet Rupert at the door naked and wrapped in plastic."

Pastor Goforth blows the image of a naked Tizzie Dearstone out his nose.

"The second I saw Marabel Morgan's face smiling up at me out of that dresser drawer, I knew it was a sign from God. I read that book from cover to cover three times and I memorized some parts," Tizzie says, taking the book out of Pastor Goforth's lap to show him the passages about how to make your husband feel special, how to organize housework, how to communicate and listen. "But, best of all is the chapter on how to enjoy sex."

Pastor Goforth thinks Tizzie is the shyest person in his congregation. She and Rupert always sit on the back, right pew near the door, and Tizzie often dashes out pulling Rupert behind her before Pastor Goforth can march from the pulpit to the receiving line. Now, he does not know what to say to the new Tizzie sitting before him.

"Tizzie Dearstone, I believe you are in God's good hands," he finally says. He blows his nose again.

"No other woman's going to get my Rupert," says Tizzie. "He's a skinny little feller and not much to look at, but he's mine and I love him."

Tizzie puts out more donuts from a Magic Dough box. "I've seen the women next door and across the street a-going and a-blowing. I know they're talking about me. I can see in Grace's eyes she don't think much of me because I'm fat. Now, I don't care about that. It's a shame me and Rupert never got to know everybody around here too well, but I was always embarrassed about my size, and I thought people would make fun of Rupert being married to me." Tizzie sucks sugary syrup off her thumb in three little pops of her mouth. "But the truth is that Rupert likes me fat. He says it's like having three wives all in one."

Tizzie insists that Pastor Goforth take Marabel Morgan's book and read it. "It's an old book, but it could do a lot of good in your line of work," Tizzie says, shaking Pastor Goforth's hand. "You ought to put one of these books between the hymnal and the Bible in every pew."

"Well, Tizzie. If you and Rupert can stay out of the bedroom for an hour or so on Sunday mornings, we'd sure like to see you back in church again." Pastor Goforth is astonished at what he has heard himself say. He puts his handkerchief back in his pocket.

Mamie lights another cigarette. A pile of ashes and six short stubs lie mashed in S-shapes on the saucer. "You never can tell." Mamie shakes out the match. "Some men like meat on their woman."

Mamie's remark makes Sandra recall a centerfold poster she once saw in Odell's girlie magazine that he'd left under their mattress. She had been spring cleaning and moved the mattress to dust the springs. Sandra's mother had given them the springs to start housekeeping, and Sandra had to clean the old fashioned metal coils with a coneshaped duster, one at a time. Sandra remembers being shocked that Odell would look at a *naked book*, as her mama called them. Lying across the bed springs, a nude blond with breasts the size of two ripe cantaloupes smiled from the magazine cover.

"What could a happily married man see in such trash," she thought to herself. Sandra thumbed through the magazine. Nude women lay in grotesque poses, their lips parted and their eyelids half shut. The middle spread of the magazine featured a large centerfold titled *Fat But Nice*, the picture of a huge, blond woman squatting on a beach blanket at the ocean, her large thighs and haunches smooth and golden. Her breasts were the size of watermelons. "Enough woman for an army," Sandra thought.

Sandra's Grandmamma Hayes had always said that the naked human body was about the ugliest thing on earth, and if a woman wanted to keep her man, she'd buy long dresses and pull the covers to her chin of a night. Sandra had taken her grandmother's advice. Now it occurred to her that Odell didn't care whether he saw her naked anymore, not like when they were first married and he teased her clothes off her from under the covers, and threw them in a pile on the bedroom floor. After Sandra had finished dusting, she put the magazine back between the mattress and springs. She never said a word to Odell about it. But, now the remembrance made Sandra feel an odd combination of hurt, shame, guilt, and confusion.

"Pastor Goforth is leaving Tizzie's house," Grace says from the kitchen sink where she is washing up the cups and plates. "They're on Tizzie's front porch."

As Sandra walks toward the window to look out at Tizzie and Pastor Goforth, she has the oddest thought. "Who knows. Tizzie Dearstone might make a good centerfold." *Scarlet Encounter* stirs slightly on Tizzie's clothesline.

"I'd like to have been a fly on her wall," says Grace, parting the curtains.

Charlie

Charlie kicks the tires of his bike with the toe of his ragged Nikes, the ones he found along Interstate 181 one day when he was picking up aluminum cans, and a dead possum. He ties several empty orange bags to the handlebars so that they dangle like curtains at a window, affixes a half-rotted leather briefcase to the back of the seat, patting it and thinking of it as his saddlebags. Last, Charlie hangs a strand of twine around his neck. Charlie does not remember why he needs the twine dangling upon his chest, but placing it around his neck has become a comfortable habit. Charlie mounts his bike in John Wayne's pigeon-toed heave-ho style from the cowboy movies he is not really capable of analyzing, rather they are important images burned randomly into his brain.

Seven bells and a brass horn are attached along the handlebars from previous bicycles Charlie has owned over his 38 years. Charlie got his first bicycle for Christmas when he was six years old, a shiny red one with white tassels dangling off the handles, and a great, shiny brass bell on the right handlebar.

When Charlie outgrew his first bike, he persisted to keep the bell, adding it alongside his new bell on his new bike. The housemother, Mrs. O'Neill, at St. Mary's Orphanage where Charlie lived, was accustomed to his love of bells, and she showed him how to remove the bell from his old bike with a wrench and a screwdriver. He watched Mrs. O'Neill, chewing the tip of his tongue and carefully copying her motions with his hands in the air. He was nine.

Charlie's third bike had a horn that honked like a goose. After the chain on the third bike had come loose and clattered about the pavement, Charlie half-peddled and half-walked on his daily bicycle rides until the soles of his shoes burned off his feet from scooting them along the streets of Dixon, along the parking lots of stores, down alleyways, and up and down Interstate 181 from the Kroger parking lot to the north edge of town.

A woman named Ethel Wood who knew Charlie's parents before they were killed in an automobile accident on Highway 181, and who knew Charlie because he was always in the Kroger's parking lot looking around cars and in trash bins for aluminum cans to put in his orange bags, bought him his fourth bike. Ethel Wood had children, and grandchildren. She had watched Charley riding his bike, pushing with one foot, dragging with the other almost like a scooter, and she had studied Charlie for shopping days on end, watching him gaze worshipfully at the new bikes lined up outside the K-Mart. She watched as Charlie marched back and forth along the line of chained bikes with his back straight, his hands locked behind him like a general weighing up his troops, his shoe-soles coming loose from the leather, his toes bloodied and scabbed black from scooting his broken bike with his feet.

But it was Charlie's beautiful face, his perfectly formed body, his mind locked up in permanent childhood that moved Ethel Wood most. Unclothed, Charlie could have been cast in Michelangelo's Pieta, the soft blue eyes, damp hair, aquiline nose, innocent and suffering, but unaware.

Charlie kept Ethel Wood's bike for seven years, a Raleigh ten-speed with all three brass bells and the honking goose horn fastened at even intervals along the handlebars. Charlie did not know to thank Ethel Wood who paid for the bike, and who supervised the K-Mart manager as he unchained it from the line and handed it to Charlie. He was twenty-two then.

Charlie has had four other bikes since, some made from parts of other bikes, some given to him. And now, the seven bells, and the honking horn, whose throat has long since sung like a goose, rides mutely on the bars beside the bells that tinkle and chime in Charlie's ears. Chime like church music.

And so each morning Charlie arranges himself with his ropes around his neck and his bicycle with the orange bags, and two orange University of Tennessee football pennants floating above either side of his handlebars on car antennas. Charlie replaces the saddlebag behind the seat each day after he has collected dead animals along the roadsides and ditches, and made for them a final resting place.

Charlie does not think about his day's work or make detailed plans.

No need. Charlie's life grows inevitably out of his routine. His days accumulate, like the pockets and buttons that Charlie sews on his worn denim jacket and overalls, sewn over and around the existing pockets. Sewn from pockets and buttons that people give to Charlie, or from ones Charlie finds in the odd places that only he knows about. Places like the dumpster behind Jacobs' Tailoring and Repair in an alley off Market, dumpsters behind the Wylie Dixon Mall, and the back entrance to the county morgue where Mr. Arthur gives him the clothing off car crash victims, and Doughty-Robbins Funeral Home where he is sometimes given false teeth out of a box full of them in the director's office. Charlie is allowed to select them himself. He sews the teeth around the headband of his ball cap.

Charlie fills his pockets with things. Pennies. Pop tops off aluminum cans. These become his rings. Unusual and shiny stones. Broken pieces of glass. Green, blue, red. Good colors to keep in pockets. Charlie chooses small things that amuse him to look at, to feel, to keep buttoned safely inside his pockets. He rubs the buttons on his pockets like worry stones between his fingers as he rides his bike. The rubbing makes his mouth water.

Dogs like Charlie. Stray dogs, particularly. Six or eight of them routinely troop behind Charlie's bike. They trot like cavalry to the smooth roll of tires, the tinny clank of aluminum cans, the flapping orange pennants high above Charlie's handlebars, the tingling bells. A Shepherd, a long-haired mixed breed, a Chihuahua, a terrier of sorts, a small scabby orange dog with three legs, and other varieties have adopted Charlie. Charlie and the dogs ride and trot together in happy circles around the grocery store parking lot, around and around like a kite of man and bicycle, and a ribbon-tail of dogs, circling from the top of the hill where the grocery is, down toward the dumpsters and recycling bins at the bottom of the parking lot, and back around again.

The dogs take turns sniffing the dead possum in Charlie's deteriorating saddlebag behind the bicycle seat. The possum's swollen tail dangles. The hungry dogs do not growl and tear at the animal, rather they seem to show reverence for Charlie's dead possum, and do no more than sniff.

Sometimes people are rude to Charlie as he rides his bike around the parking lot. A teenaged boy calls to him, "Road-Kill Cowboy."

Charlie waves back and smiles. Sometimes people swerve their cars to miss Charlie and the dogs, or they complain to the grocery store manager about the smells, or a child is frightened of the button-man with his clothes of many pockets. Someone from the grocery comes out waving a rolled-up grocery ad, and shoos them away.

Most people pay no attention to Charlie riding the roads, or the grocery store parking lot. His presence has grown as familiar to them as a tree or a fence post or the grocery store itself. And since people do not speak to trees or fences, neither do they speak to Charlie. Charlie has no realization that he has become as routine a thing as the landscape. He is riding the air like a kite. Sometimes his eyes are closed against the wind, the memory of the road an instinct in his hands upon the handlebars, the bicycle bells church music chiming in his ears.

Only a few people know Charlie, who he really is; those who feed him. Evenings, Charlie eats at the back door of St. Mary's Catholic School for Girls that used to be the orphanage where he grew up, but has since become a day school. Charlie is enormously attracted to the brass buttons and roomy jacket pockets on the girls' uniforms, and that is why he is no longer allowed to come inside and eat at the dining room table.

Once when he was twelve, he pulled the buttons off Jeanette McCarty's coat, sending the young girl into a screaming fit. When the buttons resisted, Charlie put one hand on Jeanette's breast and pulled with the other hand. When the buttons still resisted, Charlie put his mouth over each button and bit them off, as Jeanette laid screaming and kicking on the floor. When the house mother tried to take the buttons away from Charlie, he swallowed them.

Charlie eats lunch every day at the Dixon High School cafeteria. Every day at 12:00 noon, Mrs. Zelda, the cook, in her white uniform and netted hair, comes to the back door of the cafeteria and hands out a Styrofoam plate of leftovers. She sets her nose in the air sniffing the wind like a hound.

"What is that awful smell, Charlie?" Charlie puts his nose into the wind like Mrs. Zelda, but he does not answer because he does not talk. "Charlie, you've got a dead animal again," she points her blunt finger at the satchel. "Ripe as a bacon factory, I'd say." Charlie shares his bread with the dogs. They lick his plate and his dirty hands. Mrs. Zelda swishes her white apron at Charlie sending him and the dogs away, her fingers pinching her nose together. She can not know that the smells of dead and rotting things are quite acceptable to Charlie.

"Irma Jean Reagan would turn over in her grave if she could see you, Charles Percival Reagan, come to picking up dead animals all over God's creation, and come to living with the dogs on the street." Mrs. Zelda prays under her breath, "God, preserve us from perverse and unnatural things."

Charlie does not always live on the street, although sometimes a mattress thrown into an alley, or a leafy mound under some tree, will do nicely for him and the dogs. In the winter, Charlie may live at the county poor farm, or at the Haven of Mercy on Market Street, whichever he should wander into.

In summer, Charlie lives in the rusted shell of a tiny house trailer that sits behind an abandoned textile factory on the south edge of Dixon. All around the abandoned factory is a high fence overgrown with honeysuckle and trumpet vine. The front grounds are littered with trash where the homeless crawl under the broken gate to sleep, or fight, or hide. On the back side of the factory, the trailer, once used for a construction office, sits in the shadow of the high brick building with huge rock-splattered windows.

Inside the rusting hull of the trailer are high pyramids of aluminum cans, stacked neatly, row upon row, Coca-Cola, 7-UP, Pepsi, Canada Dry, Mountain Dew, and other brands, neatly sorted and built into individual monuments. Charlie chooses a Mountain Dew monument for the dead possum. The resting place is dug at the end of a long row of other metal monuments behind the factory. The possum will rest beside the dead puppy Charlie found on the Wylie Dixon Highway the week before. The row of monuments stretches in one long, continuing line across the back lot of the building.

Charlie does not know why the tin monuments are important to him. But somewhere beyond memory, Charlie carries the imprint in his mind of the day a tall man in dark robes walked toward him down a concrete pathway, the black hem swinging around his shoes, the white stole fastened around his neck, and nearly touching the hem of his vestments. St. Mary's Church is superimposed against the hill behind the man, the tall spires ring out music. The sky and trees are singing.

The man in vestments holds out his hand, but Charlie is afraid of this man towering above him whose black-clad body seems cavernous and dark as a grave against the blue sky. His cold hands smell like roses. His stone face does not smile.

A breeze touches Charlie's face like the fingers of Mrs. O'Neill. She is walking behind them. Charlie looks back over his shoulder and sees her prayerful and solemn, not trusting the familiar clacking of her footsteps on the concrete walk for assurance that she is really there.

Then at the end of the long walk is the wrought iron gate screeching open, before Charlie, and the robed man, and Mrs. O'Neill, and after that, the cemetery. Marble crosses, stone statuary, monolithic headstones, are laid out before them in rows and rows, neat and orderly, stretching across the hillside.

Charlie walks on the leash of the man's arm, slightly behind, stepping sideways now and then to push the windy robe out of his face with his free arm, winding around a statue of Mary whose cracked smile confuses him, threading between a row of haw trees, on and on between the rows of head stones and pots of flowers, between freshly dug mounds and sunken places alike, an infinite place of order and permanence.

Finally, at the curve of the hill are two neatly dug graves, and mounds of red dirt partially covered by tarpaulins. People wearing black stand silently with their hands clasped before them. Charlie, out of breath, squints into the sunshine, and looking down the vast hillside, sees the rows of headstones shimmering like long silver ribbons, and when he holds his breath and squints a certain way into the sun, he, too, is floating with the ribbons of light. This is the beginning.

To Boldly Go

When my old man, Eddie, gets drunk, he listens with his ear against things. The floor. A plate. The eggbeaters. The light bulb in the kitchen ceiling. Eddie got up on the step ladder to listen to the light bulb. It almost burned his ear lobe off. I could smell Eddie cooking when I knocked him off that ladder. Last night I came off the night shift from the Road Runner Market and found Eddie listening to my Teflon frying pan, his head down and his eyes closed like he was sleeping on a pillow. I dropped my pocketbook on the floor and screamed. "God. Eddie's frying his head!" But I checked and the stove wasn't on. See, when Eddie is drunk and listening to things, he doesn't think about turning the light bulb off, or the stove eye on. He only thinks about putting his ear against some object and listening, for hours and hours.

Like the time the chickens got into the bedroom wall. Eddie claims he can see what he's listening to. The chickens laid mounds of golden eggs, so shiny they made his eyes hurt. A big hairy hand came out of nowhere and wrung their necks, snap-crackle like dry branches, heads hanging limp as wilted flowers, chicken eyes open and dead.

Eddie could see the dead chickens jump onto a barbed wire fence, roosting, with hooked beaks and broken heads flopping. Suddenly, Eddie heard blue sky everywhere, and he heard thousands and thousands of chickens clucking on the wire, stretched in one line as long as the universe. The chickens had no more worries or miseries, roosting forever, in the dark blue of outer space. That's how Eddie described it.

Eddie was kneeling upon the bed with his knees and his right ear against the wall like he was mourning against a dead relative's casket.

"Lord, Eddie." I stood by the foot of the bed and rubbed his shoulder. "It's cockroaches you're hearing crawling around through the dry wall. We'll have the bug man come, Eddie, and you won't have to listen to the roaches anymore."

Eddie's head came away from the wall. Drunk as he was, he knocked me back through the bedroom door before I saw his fist coming at me. I landed square on my rear end on the kitchen floor and slid into the sink cabinet.

Eddie screamed from the bedroom, "By damned, Myra, I do know a chicken from a cockroach."

I couldn't get off the floor for twenty minutes. After I turned sixty, my bones got brittle and my back got sore, and it got harder to take Eddie's whacks like I did when I was younger. But, never mind, I tried to comfort my old man, sprawled on my backside in the kitchen floor and him slobbering drunk in the bedroom.

I've always been talking through walls to Eddie, seems like. I've always been talking around doors and shouting over my shoulder and across the table, and sometimes talking right up in Eddie's face. He don't hear a thing I say, like he's in some far off place where he can only see the things he's listening to in the walls and the frying pan. Sometimes I think I ought to sit inside a liquor bottle, let Eddie drink me down. I could shout at him from inside his guts or his brains, instead of shouting from the kitchen floor.

"You think you heard chickens because we worked all those years in the chicken factory. Remember that? Their heads was gone when they came off the truck. You got chicken factory memories all mixed up with the cockroaches running around in the walls."

"By damned. I know a chicken from a cockroach!" Eddie's tears rolled down his cheeks and made the front of his shirt wet. He'd make you think a drunk really has feelings.

Eddie lost his job at the chicken factory on a real sunny day in late summer. It was 1983, I believe. I've thought back on that day a lot lately, and I know that was exactly the day Eddie started losing his marbles. Eddie was working in feathers that day. Jobs at the plant were rotated so people wouldn't get bored and do sloppy work. Some days we plucked, some days we gutted, and some days we scooped the dead chickens out of the washing pond where they all floated together in bloody bath water. We laid the chickens on a moving belt and they went around to another part of the factory for cutting and packaging.

Eddie was running the chickens through a machine that beats off the feathers. After that he stuffed the feathers in sacks to be washed, dried, and packed off to bedding companies to make expensive feather pillows. Eddie couldn't stand the feathers. He took a sneezing fit that wouldn't stop. We tried mashing fingers under his nose. We stuffed his head into a brown grocery bag. We tried scaring him. He pinched his nose and drank two quarts of water. Nothing stopped his sneezing.

Edna Wannamaker, who has been at that chicken factory over thirty years, rears out of a nest of feather bags and says, "Go out and gaze into the sun, Eddie. Looking into light is a cure for sneezing."

Eddie went out to the gravel parking lot, and looked straight into the burning sun. He stopped sneezing. But something funny happened to Eddie. He couldn't stop staring into the sun. He was hypnotized.

"Eddie. You're going to go blind." I put my hands over his eyes.

Eddie pulled my hands away from his face and said the strangest thing. "Myra? Wonder what a man could see between here and the sun?"

I looked up toward the eyeball-burning sun, studied a minute. "Looks to me like its empty as a beggar's bucket."

And then Eddie's face glazed over, a sweat popping up through his white whiskers where he hadn't shaved for a day or two, his red eyes rimmed up with water. "Well, one of these days I'm going to go out there and see for myself." He walked back inside, picked up a dead chicken out of the cooler box and plucked feathers like jerking hair out of a doll's head.

Eddie sneezed so hard and fast his head shook like a rattler. He'd go look at the sun and come back to the feathers. Eddie wasn't just looking up at the sun every time he visited the parking lot, though. He was swigging off a bottle of Jim Beam hidden under the front seat of the car. Eddie came in walking crooked and talking slurry, his face dark as a beet pickle. Eddie puffed his chest like a bullfrog, walked over to Johnny Brody, the supervisor, and demanded to be put on gutting. "I ain't taking them damned feathers any more. Put me on the gutting machine."

Johnny Brody spoke only once, like your daddy did. He was a big man with powerful hands, towering over everybody. He ruled the chicken factory with an iron will. He didn't expect trouble from his workers, and he didn't get trouble. Johnny walked forward until his shadow fell across Eddie's face. He spoke in his megaphone voice. "Plucking is backed up, Eddie. Two refrigerated trucks with dead chickens parked in the lot. Gutting crew waiting on chickens. Get back to plucking."

The air wheezed out of Eddie's chest like a man dying, his chin fell, his eyes watered up. His lower lip quivered. "Get me out of them feathers. I'm suffocating."

"Take a Benadryl," Johnny said, "and get back to work.

Johnny barely got turned around when Eddie's face snapped open like a pocket knife. He punched Johnny in the chest. Lord knows, Eddie had backhanded me enough times, but Eddie had never turned on a big man like Johnny Brody.

When the fight started, I was working the line, grappling chickens out of the plunging pond and laying them on the conveyor belt. Eddie and Johnny were standing near the pond, it floating thick with plucked chickens and blood scum. Eddie turned Paul Bunyan strong. He picked Johnny up and pushed him under the belt line into the chicken water, and then he crawled under the line of chickens moving around the belt and jumped in on top of him. Soon as the hooking crew saw them in the chicken pond, the line stopped. Mack Jones and Sammy Watson climbed into the water and tried to stop Eddie, but they couldn't lay hold of him. Eddie had Johnny pinned below the water and his drowning breath came bubbling up through the bloody scum. I kept screaming, "Stop, Eddie!" Mack swam under that chicken water, and pulled Eddie's legs out from under him, and Sammy hauled out Johnny Brody coughing up scum and feathers.

I lost my job, too. I begged Johnny Brody, and the plant manager to let me work. I wrote a letter apologizing for Eddie. I reminded everybody in authority that me and Eddie had been working our whole married life at the chicken factory, loyal workers for twenty years.

"Hell no," said Johnny. "He's a drunk. He's out of control."

Eddie started drinking heavy after his firing, lying around the house watching TV and pissing on my couch. I got a convenience store job at The Road Runner Market on the Wylie Dixon By-Pass, and it wasn't long until I started working double shifts.

Eddie wouldn't strike a lick. He wanted us to leave Dixon, find jobs in another town far away, get a fresh start. We could pack up our old Rambler with a blanket or two, some pots and pans, a few clothes, find a new place. Eddie said we were living in a one-horse town with no future. "Close your eyes, Myra, and try to put us in a new place. Put us in Montana, big sky country. Put us on the Great Lakes. Put us in some big city. Close your eyes and see us somewhere else."

I shut my eyes to picture me and Eddie out west or up north, and lord, what I saw looked like Dixon, three red lights on the main street through town, one at the volunteer fire department and the post office, one at the New Ebenezer Presbyterian Church where I go Sundays to hear preaching when I'm not working or cleaning up after Eddie. In the dark behind my closed eyes, I'd see the shady streets, the small clapboard houses like the one we live in, the burley tobacco warehouse beside the railroad tracks, Junior Johnson's Service Station, Blue Jay Car Wash, the new Hardee's, half built. I see the Wylie Dixon Poultry Company where me and Eddie worked all those years.

I open my eyes, squint dark spots away, Eddie standing there smiling at me like he thinks I am going to tell him I will pack up and go with him. "I can't see anything but Dixon," I tell Eddie.

Eddie's open mouth breathed in and out like a fish dying. "Know what I see in Dixon, Myra? I see all them acres of ropy chicken guts spread out there across the hillside. Baking like a dead man's brains in the sun. I got to get away from them rotting brains."

"They sell the guts for cat food now, Eddie. That was years ago when they left chicken guts rotting on the hill outside town. You're not talking any sense."

I told Eddie that for my part we'd stay put. We got a comfortable little house, four rooms and a bath, left to me when my Daddy died. It's where I grew up, and where I've lived all my life. All of my dead relatives are buried in the New Ebenezer Presbyterian Cemetery. Who's going to keep their graves tended? I told Eddie I can't give up the house, and him drinking all the time. It's me putting bread on the table, and it's up to me to decide whether we'll stay or go.

I was as mad at Eddie as I've ever been and got away without a beating, but he spoke back to me in a voice as calm as pond water. "A man ought to be a chicken. Dead or alive, doesn't matter. A chicken gets to travel. A chicken moves off the farm, rides in a big truck to the chicken factory, maybe seeing hundreds of miles of scenery on the way. That chicken gets spruced up for somebody's dinner table, wearing a big name label in a fancy Styrofoam package. That chicken might get breaded into nuggets and end up at McDonald's in New York City where some famous person eats it, or it could end up in a fancy chicken pie and be shipped off to California where that chicken meets people at suppertime and does some good in his life filling empty bellies, and making people smile and lick their lips. A man ought to be a chicken."

"That chicken is dead and can't see any of the places you're talking about," I say to Eddie.

Eddie says back, "A man that can't go some place and make something of himself might as well be dead, too." Eddie's lips puckered like a baby's. "At least I can listen to places nobody else can hear."

"You're drunk, Eddie."

Eddie took a swing at me, but I ducked back a step and his fist hit the door facing. "Dammit, Myra. I know a chicken from a cockroach." Eddie got up off the bed and peed. His clothes hung dripping on him. And he'd vomited on the carpet again. I wiped it up between the threads and thin places. Thunderbird, that fruity sour smell. Cheap liquor is all Eddie buys on what few dollars he bums off his friends.

When Eddie's on a drunk, I search all his hiding places. I find his liquor bottle up the flue on a sooty ledge, or hidden under the ashes of the charcoal grill. Once I caught him swigging out of the Drano bottle. Eddie is clever at finding places to hide liquor. Last time he stayed slogged for three days, I searched in the water closet behind the commode, outside in the guttering, under the steel lid of the water meter, in the freezer, in my car. All the time Eddie was mixing cheap liquor with a gallon of fruit juice in the refrigerator. See, I hardly ever drink fruit juice on account of my ulcer, but I poured a sip and choked up a throat full of rotten stuff. You'd have to look up the cat's behind to stay ahead of Eddie.

Eddie's drinking is expensive, too. I'm still paying off doctor bills from the last time Eddie went to the sanitarium to dry out. I say, "What if you get sick and have to go to the doctor again, and it two years more before you can sign up for Medicaid and us with no insurance. You're damned lucky I'm healthy, except for this ulcer," I tell him.

It's got so when Eddie's not drunk, he's buzzed on TV, mostly watching the old Star Trek re-runs on WNOT 39. When I tell him to get his lazy butt up and find a job, he goes over and puts his head against the refrigerator and listens to the space ship, USS Enterprise, to the quiet hum of its engines floating through space, soaring gently at the speed of light to places where Eddie says no man has gone before, but where he is certain to go some day. That's what he says, anyway, looking at me with them droopy-dog eyes and his face snuggled up to the refrigerator.

"No man has gone beyond the moon because there's nothing out there," that's what I tell Eddie. "Think about the afternoon we watched the moon landing, how Armstrong plopped out of his lunar module into the dust of the moon jumping like a child in a sandbox. All that money spent on space suits and rockets so grown men can rabbit-hop in moon dust and pick up moon rocks, and that silly man, Aldrin, hitting golf balls on the moon, all the while people down on earth needing a hot meal or a warm place to live."

Every time I say this Eddie gets a far-away gaze on his face and mumbles, "A small step for man. A giant leap for mankind."

"A giant leap toward hell, Eddie. That's what. God gave us all common sense, and there was no sense in spending money on moon trips."

Eddie has never been sensible like me. Eddie said that I have a way of knowing what God thinks, and God always agrees with me. Eddie said he never could figure out what God wanted him to do. That's why he's such a grave disappointment on earth. Out there in space, it might be different.

"Just think, Myra," Eddie said, "There are women on the USS Enterprise going where no man has gone before. Even a nigger woman can go. A Russian communist and a Vulcan with pointed ears can get along together with white people and niggers alike. Isn't that what God's been talking about?"

Eddie said we can both go out there together. He'd show me how to listen myself to outer space. "See here, Myra. With your head up against the fridge, like this." I got down on my knees beside Eddie, and like a fool put my ear against our old refrigerator. The motor vibrated against the wall of the fridge, that's all I heard. With Eddie's eyes closed and his face hugged up to that fridge he looked like a child dreaming. Lord, I could have cried, but I got through the days by reminding myself that God won't put more on me than I can bear.

Only Star Trek kept Eddie calm. I rented videos so he could watch them when the reruns went off. I watched them, too, but I had to put my hands over my face and peek between my fingers because the shows scared me so bad, like the show where a big white ape with poison fangs bit Captain Kirk. Eddie said not to worry. A gypsy woman who knows all the mountain cures will lay hands on him. She's like an herbalist faith healer.

Every day, Eddie watched back-to-back Star Trek. I asked him, "Why do you want to go to all those dangerous places, Eddie?"

"Myra, there's always some monster eating up the natives, some energy gluttonous glob of matter sucking up space ships, some damned invisible mite invading the circuits. Mostly, the Klingons trying to take over the universe."

Eddie says we'll be lucky if we never meet up with the Klingons, long-haired heathens dressed up in metal and furs, going about killing, and pillaging all over space. They look like they stink and I could smell them right off the TV. Or maybe it was Eddie.

In the dead of winter Eddie got to talking peculiar. He wasn't Eddie any more. He was Kirk, Captain of the USS Enterprise. I wasn't Myra. I was that pointy-eared man, Spock. Eddie never called me Myra after the day the kitchen turned into the Enterprise. Eddie took control like a new man, ordering the kitchen chair, Chekov, to Vector 36 to intercept a Federation space station which had sent out a strange distress signal.

"It might be them damned Klingons up to something, Checkov. Set a course for 3.5." The door leading to the basement steps was the engine room. Eddie walked over to the door, tapped his shoulder. "Scotty, give me all the power you got." Eddie turned sideways and answered himself in a funny accent. "Right on, Capt'n."

"Star Date 4108," Eddie spoke to the kitchen stove, pushing the timer button, "A strange distress signal emanating from Federation space station in Vector 36. Suspect Klingons. USS Enterprise moving to intercept."

Eddie turned on his heel and ordered me. "Spock, see that we keep shields up. Remain on yellow alert. You can't trust a damned Klingon as far as you can throw one. If I find out they're up to their usual no-good, I'm going to kick them out of Federation space."

"Spock, we've got to be careful," Eddie put his hand on my shoulder, ruffled his forehead. "The Klingon vessel is probably cloaked. They're laying a trap for us. I can feel it." I didn't know this man standing in my kitchen ordering me to keep phasers on stun.

"Spock. Too bad the Federation won't let us clean out that nest of Klingon polecats once and for all. But if we kill them, we won't have any bad guys to fight tomorrow. The way of the universe, Spock.

Maintain the status quo."

I had to look up status quo in the dictionary. Keep things the way they are. I didn't know Eddie knew such a word. I knew he was smart, all right, even though he quit high school to work in the chicken factory. He used to keep his nose poked in a book or a magazine all the time, but he never talked to me about anything he was reading.

Eddie climbed from a chair to the middle of the kitchen table, the transporter room. He stood straight as an arrow, like my old Eddie, but his shirt was buttoned in the wrong holes so that it bunched at the neck and the white hair on his belly stood up in a stiff ridge. "Transporter room. Prepare to beam an away team to Federation Space Station."

Eddie looked down at me with glazed eyes, "Spock, you take over the Enterprise. If we're not back in thirty minutes, get the hell out of Dodge. We may be facing the most subversive Klingon plot yet to betray the American dream."

It was me that felt betrayed by that man standing in the middle of my kitchen table. All the years I had persevered through his drunkenness, always keeping my chin up, always plowing ahead, doing what needed to be done to survive, never grumping one minute, always climbing back up every time Eddie knocked me down, smiling through the hard times, keeping the faith. No matter. Eddie got worse.

One day I came off the day shift early with a bucket of Kentucky Fried Chicken and a loaf of bread. I was fishing through a drawer for a bread knife when I glanced up and there stood Eddie looking as white as cottage cheese.

"Watch out for them Klingons in the knife drawer!" Eddie shouted out the warning just as I picked up a bread knife, the handle was gummy with red stuff. "The Klingons are hiding in there, Spock. Be careful. Don't listen to any of that talk about their power and authority bringing control and order to the universe."

Eddie had blood soaked towels wrapped around his hands. "I've been fighting them Klingons, Spock. They're running." Eddie lifted his bloody hands. "I fought them rednecks of the universe bare handed, Spock, and I have won."

"Lord, Eddie. You've been fighting a drawer full of knives and kitchen spatulas." I was crying and shaking so hard I couldn't do a thing but stand there with my arms out toward him when he fell like a bag of kindling.

Dr. Drummond said he'd never seen anything as mangled as Eddie's hands. It took one hundred odd stitches to sew up the gashes in his palms and fingers. Some places the knives had pierced through his hands. A nurse pumped a quart of blood into his right arm. Eddie lay in that hospital bed under the white sheets, snoring with his mouth open, his hands wrapped in big white clubs of bandages. He looked beat and haggard, his eyes black rimmed and sunken in, his head shrunken up and like a turnip going bad. His mouth a dry white line in the middle of his face, his light bulb ear melted away. Eddie looked like one of them awful creatures he's always watching on TV, something from across the universe you don't recognize and you hope to god doesn't exist.

Only once he blinked his eyes and spoke. "Good old Bones."

Dr. Drummond said Eddie had DT's, delirium tremens, and that he was hallucinating. Eddie hadn't been drinking much lately, but the doctor said DT's were caused by habitual excessive drinking. For Eddie, that meant a lifetime of steady drinking and twelve years of lying around dead drunk. Eddie lay unconscious in the hospital bed for a week. After that, Dr. Drummond sent him to the state sanatorium for a month of recuperation.

That was a month of hell. I didn't know what to do with myself. I didn't have Eddie to worry about, to clean up after his mess, to fuss with about his drinking and his laziness. One day I went shopping for the first time in months. I drove to the Wylie Dixon Mall, and bought a new dress and a chicken frying skillet. I though about Eddie coming home. I'd make his favorite fried chicken in the new skillet. He'd worn the Teflon off my old skillet listening to rogue elephants in Kenya, eating the peanut crops and laughing through their snouts at anybody who tried to stop them. I threw that skillet in the trash to keep the elephants out of Eddie's head.

The new skillet was so big I left it setting on top of the stove. It was a deep, long-handled skillet with a glass domed lid. The day the county ambulance drove Eddie home, I waited at the kitchen door. Two men helped Eddie inside, but he didn't even see me. He looked around the kitchen like he was looking over the old home place, then he walked over to the skillet and said, "Spock. I see that you have maintained the Enterprise in good order during my absence."

Dr. Drummond put Eddie on Valium to keep him calm.

So I could take better care of Eddie, I switched to evening shift. Every night I put Eddie in bed, gave him two sleeping pills and went off to work. I got home in the shank of the night, caught a few hours of sleep, and watched over Eddie during the day. Eddie watched Star Trek re-runs and slept on the couch most of the time. I gave up trying to keep him neat. He didn't want me coming near him with the scissors or the razor. His hair and beard grew in long gauzy white strands. I gave him a sponge bath now and then, changed his clothes every day. I cooked his favorite foods, but he ate only a bite or two and got thinner every day. I got fatter, eating my part and his, too.

One night I didn't get in from work until after midnight. I came quietly into the dark kitchen through the back door. I thought Eddie was asleep. But there in the dim street light shining through the window I saw Eddie standing in the middle of the kitchen table holding out an empty white pillow case in each hand, and wearing my new Teflon skillet on his head like a ball cap with the bill turned to the side, the glass skillet lid smashed on the kitchen floor. I could see flecks of glass reflected where the street light hit the floor, and I told myself to be careful where I walked.

I heard Eddie's voice. "Transporter room. Prepare to beam Kirk to Federation space station." Eddie was transporting himself off again on some mission, his bare feet bleeding where he'd stepped on broken glass, the blood oozing out on my clean table top, running under the salt and pepper shakers and into the napkin holder, an orange puddle in the light.

"Lord god, above, Eddie. You've cut yourself again."

"Stand back, Spock. There's going to be a lot of dead chickens up there if I don't bring them back to earth."

I grabbed Eddie by the ankles and held on for dear life. I thought he was going to dive off the table.

"Stand back, Spock, and let me beam up. That's an order."

"You come down off the table right this minute, Eddie." I tried to threaten him, but no use.

"Stand back, Spock. Be sensible. I'm right this time, you know." Eddie's voice was soft and peaceful.

"Why must you go this time Eddie? Why don't you wait until you get to feeling better?"

"I go because it is difficult. I go because I am afraid." Eddie's voice was still as pond water. "Even you must see the logic of that, Spock."

The blast of light came into the kitchen through the windows, through my thin curtains as bright as the second coming. Light bounced off the walls, off the refrigerator, off the broken glass on the floor, from the stove eyes to the ceiling, like it was alive and searching for something. The light roared like a lion, it shook like an earthquake. Finally, the bright roar settled over Eddie standing in the middle of the kitchen table. Eddie stood in the blazing light with his arms outstretched, the pillow cases dangling from his hands, and that teflon skillet wobbling on his head.

I looked up at Eddie wrapped in brightness from the window behind him. Merciful heaven. Eddie was a scarecrow, a thin beam of wood wearing trousers cinched at the waist, the end of his belt dangling a foot. His shirt hung on the rail of his arms outstretched and holding the pillow cases. Lord, his gauzy hair lit up like cotton candy, his face gray and gaunt like somebody who has been dead for years and then dug up.

I saw light coming out of Eddie's mouth when he said, "Beam me up, Scotty." Eddie's peaceful voice seemed like it echoed out of a metal drum. He was so bright I could see through him. I could hear the big hum of engines. I could feel the vibrations shaking the kitchen windows, shaking the glasses in the cabinets, shaking right down through Eddie's ankles which seemed no bigger than broom handles.

Suddenly, the kitchen went black as midnight. I felt the dull thud of Eddie toppling off the table onto the kitchen floor, me crumpling up with him. When I finally shook sense into my head, I recognized the roar of the city garbage truck backing out of the driveway, the bright headlights backing out of my kitchen, passing over Eddie lying in a white heap.

Eddie won't be coming home again. He's now in the state sanatorium, a wisp of a man. You can barely see his feet, the knobs of his knees and his hip bones making little bumps under the white covers. Eddie's melting away like old snow. There's a strange smile frozen on Eddie's face, though, and I think he's listened himself off somewhere when I hear the gurgle in his throat. Eddie opens his mouth, slightly. The light that floats toward the ceiling is round, the size of a walnut, but clear as a bubble. It hovers ever so silently above the bed, and then it disappears into the light.

Flashpoint

I had not been dead five minutes before Riley cupped his hand over Charity Sanborn's left breast, causing her to let out a silly giggle. I watched Riley and that blond nurse he'd hired to take care of me during my last days alive on this earth, carrying on like love-struck teenagers. I could see them while I lay unconscious in my own bed at home, and Charity Sanborn tucking my covers, adjusting the feeding tube in my stomach, or the oxygen tubes in my nostrils, or wiping streaks of bile from the edges of my mouth. All that while Riley stood at my deathbed, massaging her danger zones, working his hands up her rib cages and over her breasts, rubbing his groin into her backside.

I could see all this, out of some vision I can't yet understand myself. I could see Charity Sanborn giggling and slapping at Riley. "Now, Mr. Riley. Please let me do my job." Her job was catching Riley Lambert before his wife was dead, buried, and properly mourned. I know her type, that blond vulture.

In my dying, tied to my body by threads as thin as spider webs, I watched them in living color, feeling myself busting loose from myself, one thread snapping at a time. I thought of myself as a caterpillar changing into a butterfly, as a locust leaving its shell, as an egg separating, white from yoke. "I see you Riley Lambert. I see you Charity Sanborn. You miserable, indecent sinners!"

I believe I was already dead before the doctor forced a tube down my windpipe and wired me to that machine that beeps like a false heart. I was floating outside myself already, watching, when a white light gusted me like a leaf around the hospital room. I swirled across the nurses' white uniforms, melted into the lights, rolled like a breeze from under the bed, bumped softly against walls, floors, then the ceiling, light as breath.

From the ceiling, I watched Riley standing by the emergency room door, his hands in his pockets, his shoulder against the doorframe. "Is she dead?" Riley asked the doctor in the same voice that asks, "Is dinner ready?"

I floated against the ceiling above the doctor's balding head. Then with a jagged lurch I flashed back inside myself, felt the doctor's hands pressing against my face, the tube slipping inside my throat, my right hand death-gripping a nurse's arm. My left side was as stiff and unbending as a dead tree. My blood felt like hot acid, an awful, hellish pain coursing through me. And then came the numbing cold, the left half of me frozen solid and the right half of me molten. Cold Hell and hot Hell, both.

"Marigold wouldn't want to be hooked up to those tubes. Unfasten her right now." Riley's words gonged inside the church bell of my ears, and I put my hands to my metal head to stop the vibrating, and my fingers could not find the substance of my head, and then I went where the world is tipsy, and I saw my hands drawn into clinched fists at the ends of my grey sweater sleeves.

The doctor explained to Riley that I'd be on life support until he could determine the severity of my condition.

"I don't want Marigold hooked up if she's going to be a vegetable."

"That decision can not be made yet," the doctor said.

Decision? I spiraled back along the twisted root of memory to my parents' sitting room. "You WILL marry Riley Lambert." Daddy said as Riley and I stood before him and Mama, the faces of several generations of dead relatives, aunts, uncles and grandparents, lined up on the mantle looking sternly from old black and white pictures, a long line of silent mouths set in fatal lines of resignation.

"You WILL get married." Daddy's eyes narrowed, his mind snapped shut.

"I don't want to marry Riley," I said.

In an instant, Daddy came off the settee to slap me. Mama came toward me sooner. She opened her mouth to say "NO," stepped in to catch Daddy's hand. Instead she took the blow across her face. Blood came up to the corner of her mouth. That motion picture has haunted me for thirty eight years. Now, I understand my mother, who had always kept the peace by passivity, who had lived only in that one grand second when she had turned loose of her own self-consciousness, to act from her heart.

My baby girl died at birth close after Riley and I were married. I remember the closed bud of her face, but I could not weep. In dying, I felt a closer kinship. I felt her waiting for me just beyond. Though, I could not see her.

Riley stood at the hospital room door with his head down, frozen in his boots. He would have let my daddy slap me. He would have let the doctor unhook my life. He would let Charity Sanborn make a fool of me in my own home.

I lived on in unconsciousness, but I did not live inside myself. I turned loose from my body. Floating above, I could view myself from any angle I chose, see my x-rayed bones moving in the fluid sac of my flesh. I could see through the architecture of the hospital, like the rooms of a doll's house. Eventually, I learned to *think* the irrational walls back to solid again. You can not know this now, but in the beginning was the *thought*. Then came the *word*.

Hovering over my bed, I saw my body below me, plump, middle-aged, my chin fixed hard. My jowls hung slack. My eyelids floated half-opened. White tape fastened a tube that ran into my nose. An IV protruded from the large vein on the top of my hand. Wires ran from patches on my body to a monitor where my heart bleeped in thin red lines. The nurses had taken off my garden shoes, my striped dress, and wrapped me in one of those white gowns that tie in the back.

When Riley brought my body home to escape the ruin of hospital bills, I followed. Riley turned the living room into a death room, this arrangement for convenience. All the bedrooms were upstairs.

Hired to care for me, Charity Sanborn came in starched white, carrying two suitcases. She took my husband Riley in the first sweep of her eyes, and then she took my home in the blinking. Charity had bleached hair worn neatly pinned under her nurses' cap. Her huge breasts pivoted like cannons on a battlefield. She wore an iron maiden bra with double cross supports. I judged her to be my age, fifty-five. I x-rayed the lines under her makeup. Mutton done up as lamb.

Riley brought her to my bedside. "My goodness. Marigold surely is too young to be in such a state." Charity set herself to work immediately checking my tubes, adjusting my pillow, studying the features of the comatose woman. She hovered above me. I hovered above her.

Charity Sanborn seemed too big for the room, one of those people who suck up all the air. I held myself above her. Riley didn't take his eyes off her as she moved around my death bed in her scrubbed efficiency.

Charity brushed my hair. Oh, nursely soldier that she was. My hair had gone grey. No more trips to the beauty parlor. Dying is not supposed to be beautiful, is it? Charity struggled the brush through the matted, tangled mess that she called "deathbed hair." Riley brought a pair of scissors and said, "Cut the tangles out."

"Now, Mr. Riley," Charity said. "I can untangle your wife's hair. See. I'll start here at the ends of her hair and work toward the roots." After the brushing, Charity put my hair in a short braid and made iron grey spit curls upon my forehead. She powdered my face on either side of the oxygen tubes running into my nose. She painted my lips. She rouged my cheeks, making me up for her casket. Charity bade Riley approve of me with her false cheerfulness, with her petting of the blankets. He smiled his little crooked smile while I viewed my grotesque reflection in his eyes.

Charity's everlasting goodwill and patience stamped itself upon Riley. He hated seeing me withering away in my deathbed, but loved how Charity cared that I was dying. I floated upon the wall behind my bed. I watched Charity adjust the morphine pump, change my soiled diaper. I studied her false smile, the way her eyes circled back to see if Riley was watching her, and I understood that she was conscious of her own deceit.

"The least we can do is make Marigold comfortable during her final days," said Charity. I hated her calling me Marigold. I hated her reducing my authority to that of a child's.

My final days? I saw lights during my final days. Flashes of light. Polka dotted lights. Tornadoes of light. The lights were coming for me. I wanted to turn completely loose and go. I could not think myself loose from life. I could not think myself loose from Riley.

"Will she hang on much longer?" Riley said. "I mean will Marigold have to suffer this way much longer? Like a vegetable?"

"You can never really tell, Mr. Riley," Charity said. She called my husband Mr. Riley. Oh, she knew every ingratiating trick. Mr. Riley? Respectful, but personal. "I'll know the signs, Mr. Riley. Short of that we must be patient." Charity Sanborn needed me alive. She needed time to make Riley dependent upon her. I understood Charity Sanborn's motives as well as she did.

You must separate yourself from your own body in order to understand things clearly. But you can not know that now. What if I tell you that you will stay married for thirty eight years to a man because you don't know how to leave? You think that he will change. He never does. He thinks that you will always stay the same. You never can. Meanwhile, you live in the illusion of habit. Eating Cheerios for breakfast, watching re-runs of the Andy Griffith Show, packing his favorite peanut butter and dill pickle sandwiches in his lunch box, getting your flu shots each fall, paying the electric bill, buying groceries, voting, reading the newspapers, making pot roast for Sunday dinner. Living is a comfortable illusion. The things of your heart that scream out to be heard are pressed down and packed away inside you like old linens. Time passes at the bottom of the drawer. Time stands still in the rush of daily routine. Then, you are on your knees in the dirt, gouging out the stubborn roots of a cow vine that has smothered the begonias, wondering if the meat loaf in the oven should be attended, and, suddenly, the sun goes into eclipse, and the life you thought you never really wanted ends in the flower bed.

You would be surprised to know that many other women besides Charity Sanborn wanted Riley, too. Well-meaning widows from the church came with coconut cake and beef Stroganoff, bearing their special recipes before them like sacrificial gifts to the altar. But Charity had staked the territory of Riley's heart for herself. She never allowed these women to cross the threshold. If they stood tip-toe to peek inside the house, Charity squared her shoulders and leaned forward like a Mac Truck. "Mr. Lambert isn't home," she'd say, even if Riley was upstairs reading the newspaper. "Mr. Lambert doesn't want visitors. Marigold is in a coma. This ordeal is difficult enough for him." Charity made their coming seem inconsiderate. She closed the door abruptly, leaving them standing with their soufflé dishes in hand. Charity understood they'd have to return to pick up their bowl, therefore, they should not be allowed to enter. Two birds. One stone.

Did I say that Charity rearranged my furniture to suit her own taste? "You know, Mr. Riley, that sideboard would really look better against that wall," she'd say. In a flash, Riley had the house turned completely around. Charity made sure he'd switched his bedroom furniture to the spare room on the opposite end of the house. A new room. A new woman. No flashbacks from a previous bedroom allowed.

Did I tell you that Charity Sanborn sold my heirlooms to an antiques dealer, to a Mrs. Biddle, a short, stocky woman, a friend of Charity's? She came wearing a shabby raincoat and carrying an absurd umbrella with ducks quacking around the edge. She bought my doll collection for a fraction of its value. She paid a song for my trundle bed, for my great-grandmother's butter churn, the wooden dough bowl, for all my family treasures. Riley called these pieces of my heritage "the junk of the past." Charity agreed the house would look less cluttered. I had no need for these things, now, she said. I needed Riley to want to cling to something that I cherished. Maybe I could love him then, even if that meant vegetable love.

When Charity and Riley first knew the heat of their luxurious passion, I learned to blow cold. Riley first came to her bedroom after she had conveniently bumped into him in the dark hallway, her timing always perfect. She wore a see-through negligee. Her eyes spoke volumes. His eyes electrified the night. While they wallowed in the upstairs hallway, I thought myself into an icy blast. I traveled up Charity's spine and down the crevices of her huge bosom. "Eeeeeeee," she screamed and shivered. Riley must have thought she screamed for him until I rushed inside his mouth and blew at the back of his throat and came out his nose as frozen fog. And then I traveled to regions below and froze an icicle there. Charity bounced him off, screaming.

"It's her!" she said. "She's here!" Charity took Riley under the warmth of her covers and explained death to him. She had cared for the dying many times. "A doppelganger," she called me. He seemed uncomfortable with the idea that I might be loosed from my body, watching him after all, like God invisible. "Not to worry," she told him, "Not to be afraid of the cold." Charity took me on, a contest of wills. She openly courted Riley, brought his hands to her private places, even at my deathbed, and smiled at the empty room.

Perhaps you think that in the topsy-turvy space of death there is forgiveness. You can not know this now, but in your dying state all of your suppressed anger will rise green and ugly like a dead frog to the top of the cistern. You will look upon the waters and see your own ugly face. But this viewing is not like looking into a mirror. Your mirror image is but a pantomime of yourself, every movement a synchronized counter movement in the looking glass. In death, you will observe yourself in the same way you observe the grocery boy bagging your food, in the same way you observe the woman while she is stealing your husband. While she is suctioning the bile from your throat and he comes up behind her and he is thrusting his hands up the back of her white uniform to find her place of heat. While she is standing at your bed, unbuttoning her uniform, smiling down on you because she knows that you know. While your husband is having his way with the woman who is charged with keeping you alive, you die a different death. The death of the body is a simple matter compared to the death of spirit. Or had you not thought the spirit dies, too? Oh, that death is as sharp as the serpent's tooth. Oh, Death, thou art mighty and great!

I wanted to harm Charity. I wanted to gouge her eyes, yank out her hair, drive a needle into her eye, curse her with boils, bite off her ears. But in the end, my pathetic assaults were simply cold air, an inconvenience at the back of her neck.

I expected Charity to dilute the sludge-food that gurgled through the feeding tube into my stomach, fiddle with the oxygen, or pump the morphine too many times. Charity, however, was tediously patient and careful. Her uprightness impressed Riley all the more. Meanwhile, the days waxed and waned, the seasons of planting and growing had long passed. In early fall, I died the second and final time when the sign was in the heart, when that which has been uprooted can never grow back again.

Charity called Riley into the death room one evening. "Our Marigold is leaving us." She wiped at false tears. "You won't be needing me much longer, Mr. Riley."

By now I had shrunken to the size of a child, my body curled into the fetal position, blood settled into my eye sockets and turned dark, my mouth gaped wide open, my lips stretched across my teeth, the final howl on my face.

Letting go isn't easy. You might think it is, but you will stitch the last thread of your willpower to the people in the very room you hate, to the faces, the arms, the lives of the very people you hate. You will cling to the bedpost, to the furniture, to the tree outside your window, to the mailbox, to the neighbor's garden hoe, to the fence beyond the park.

No use. No use. The umbilical cord of life stretches so impossibly thin you're sure it will snap, and yet, you float farther, and farther away, and farther still, not ever breaking completely free.

A Christmas Mourning

Thomas Peach took down the rifle from the pegs above the mantle. Then, catching the drift of his own mind, he lofted it back. His wife, Julie, lay dead in the next room in her child birthing bed. He did not yet know that grief was not so easily killed; not like a black bear that can be shot down in the woods. Instead, he went outside to the shed and laid hold of the ax handle. He stopped to whet the ax on the flint wheel, the sparks arcing from the edge of the blade like a sparkling stick. Then in broad, heavy strides, he made his way along the path through the pines until he reached a stand of dead chestnut trees. He wore a red flannel shirt, sleeves rolled to the elbows. He had forgotten to put on his coat. The pines were already dusted with snow, and the cup of the valley was filling up white below the mountain.

Thomas studied the chestnuts, leafless and gray among the pine forest. He decided to cut one that had died in mid-growth. All along the mountain slopes the chestnuts were dying of blight. All the chestnuts along the Blue Ridge would be dead in another year or two. The dead and dying chestnuts, sapless and grey as skeletons, made Thomas angry. He intended to cut the dying trees down. Every last one of them, until the mountain suffered the bareness of them as the death of his wife had made his heart bare and miserable.

Nothing could be done for Julie. The blood would not be stopped. Granny Older had come with herbs and prayers. She had done all any granny woman could have done for Julie Peach. She had boiled water to throw the germs on the ceiling. She had bound Julie's belly tight with white strips of a sheet, and packed her empty womb with white rags. "Pressure," Granny Older said. "We need to bear down on that bleeding." Julie felt the blood flowing out of her like a warm river. She wondered if her own mother had felt the knowing of death before it came, as she had bled to death after Julie's birth. Julie was praying about this when the darkness came. Granny Older laid the silver dollars upon Julie's eyes, the ones she carried out of habit in her coat pocket, and then she pulled the quilt across Julie's face.

Thomas Peach did not own a cow, and a new baby to be fed. "I'm going to Dorthea Finley's and bring her to come feed the baby," the old woman had said to him as he stood at the door with the gun in his hands. Dorthea was nursing a six month old. She'd have mother's milk for this baby. It was an hour's walk to the Finleys' in good weather. "No use in taking a newborn to Dorthea and it bitter cold," she said. Granny Older wondered if she could persuade Dorthea to trudge back up the mountain, the snow filling everything up, and Christmas so near. The light would be gone by the time she got back. "I'll be back when I come," Granny said to Thomas. She looked back and saw him studying the gun, bottling up a red hot anger that was bound to explode in time.

"You're supposed to know what to do, you granny women," Thomas said to her.

"Some women bleed," said the old woman, pulling on the heavy burr coat, and wrapping her head in a wool scarf.

Thomas Peach left the child alone in the house to go outside and stare into the trees. Before leaving, Granny Older had wrapped Julie's baby in a quilt piece and tucked her into a dresser drawer, then set it before the fireplace, near enough to the fire that the light flickered across her face. The child's tight fists fought their way to the bud of its mouth. The child sucked wildly on the air. Thomas heard the crying even into the stand of chestnuts. He stopped to listen. It sounded like a kitten lost from its mother. The crying came from the house, but the sound flitted like a ghost in the pines, and then melted toward the valley.

Granny Older was the one who lifted the child from the crook of Julie's arm and straightened her body before the hardening came. At the end, it was not Thomas that Julie wanted, but the child. "I want to tell her how much I love her," Julie said to Thomas. She wanted to tell her daughter that the mother dying was no fault of the child's. Hadn't Julie bourn the guilt for her own mother's death? Whenever the family aunts gathered at Thanksgiving or Christmas, or for summer picnics, they reminded Julie that her mother had died giving birth. Her mother's death was a sacrifice so that Julie might live, they said. They spoke as if the mother's death was a thing Julie had some power over. Wasn't it God who decided these things?

"This is God's will," Julie whispered to the girl child in the crook of her arm.

Thomas wished it could be the baby dying instead of Julie. He and Julie could have bourn that grief together. There could be more children if the one died.

"I won't have you spiting the child," Julie said to Thomas at the end, seeing his eyes and heart lock against the baby, grinding his jaw the way he did when words he wanted to say he must hold back. His hand felt the warm circle of blood widening in a red halo around Julie's body. The smell startled him.

Thomas Peach took up his ax. The full force of his anger came in a swift throw into the tree. Soon he had cut a wedge into the trunk. Nearly half way through, he changed positions in the downhill side and cut a wedge so that the weight of the tree toppled it. The tree moaned as it gave way and fell in a long sob, crashing downhill between several other large chestnuts. He marked two more chestnuts and brought them down in the same way. When he stopped for a breath, a cold rush of wind shuttered up the valley and settled into the damp of his sweaty shirt. The winter sun hanging low behind the grey clouds cast an eerie light behind the bare heads of the trees.

Behind him on the hill stood the dark house, the boards weathered grey and rotting in some places, a sharecropper's house, free to live in if he could farm the hilly land and make enough to share with Walter Jenkins who owned it. He and Julie had glued newspapers over the inside walls to seal out the drafts. He had patched the floorboards as best he could with planks from a collapsed barn. He had mud-daubed between the chimney rocks and found a better pipe to line the flue so the house wouldn't catch fire. Thomas and Julie Peach were happy in this house.

Thomas had not thought to light the candles before setting out to cut down the chestnuts. The fire must be low by now. He should go back to pitch a log on the fire. Something nameless gripped him so fiercely he could not move. He could not breathe. He was as dark and empty inside as a cave.

Dorothea was too sick to travel, and Granny Older came home across the snowy mountain alone. At the crest of a slope, she caught sight of Thomas standing at the top of the hill. She stopped to catch her breath, setting her split basket on a stump beside the path. All the men were wearing the red flannel these days. Too bold a color for a man or a woman. Unseemly, she thought. Julie had bought Thomas the shirt. "Christmas is coming a week from today," she said. The two of them walked down the mountain to the Birdsong Store in Dixon to buy coffee and sugar, to buy molasses for making a gingerbread cake, to buy each other a gift. She wanted him to wear the red flannel shirt. "It makes your hazel eyes turn true brown," she said, studying his eyes like their changing from green-gold to brown with the shirt held to his chin was some kind of magic. He had bought Julie a new dress for her Christmas present. The shorter styles were coming in. Mrs. Birdsong had gone against the better advice of her neighbors and stocked a few of the new fashions.

Old Elmer Turnbull was at the Birdsong Store that afternoon, staggering beside the open bushels of dried pinto beans. He was early into his Christmas drinking. He wore a string around his neck dangling a bunch of mistletoe. He staggered to where Julie stood holding the dress and put his hands against her belly, gobbling words like an old Jake turkey. "Laws, a baby," he said. "Laws, a baby." Thomas took the old man by his collar and threw him across some sacks of dried beans. "Get away from her!" Thomas said. The old man drew himself into a ball, his face folded like a wilting flower, a question in his eyes.

"He only wants to feel the baby move," said Julie. "He don't mean any harm."

Thomas spent the tobacco crop on the dress and the red shirt worrying whether they could make it until summer and the garden came in. He didn't speak his fears to Julie. To his mind, a woman was not supposed to worry about such things as money.

Thomas Peach's red shirt glowed like a beacon in the snowy light. Granny Older yoo-hooed. She yoo-hooed again. She thought that Thomas might come and heft the basket for her, but he had turned back up the hill. Closer to the house, she caught sight of the tree branches thrashed across the path. The woods were clogged with the limbs of the dead chestnuts Thomas had struck down. She'd have to turn right and pick her way along the slope, then work her way back around to the path, and the woods filling up with quiet snow. "Lord, a man don't have sense when he needs it most," she thought. She had watched many a man handle grief by cutting trees, chopping and stacking a cord of wood, milking the cows, throwing hay to the livestock, fetching in the buckets of water. She had known a man who killed hogs when his son died of the diphtheria. It was as if a man's anger and confusion could be transformed into something tangible and useful. It could be handled, stacked, organized, and fitted into place.

A woman knew how to accept and go on better than a man. A woman knew to wait until the day closed, the children in bed asleep, the husband satisfied and snoring on his side, only the night sounds of crickets and the creaking planks of the house to meditate on. This is the time of letting go of grief, sobbing so quietly and still no one hears her private sorrows spoken into her pillow, her hands clinching and un-clinching until she lets go of her heart and falls asleep. This is the way of women, Granny Older knew.

The calves of Granny's legs throbbed as they cooled. She'd better move while she had strength. The burning cold air pumped into her lungs. Her chest ached. She couldn't feel her fingers around the basket handle. "I'm too old to be climbing these hills much longer," she thought. She shifted the basket to her left arm and pulled herself up the steep bank by gripping some ropy saplings. She worked her way around the fallen tree by digging her feet into the snow, one after the other. In this way she climbed to the Peach house.

Thomas Peach lit candles and placed one at either end of the mantle. A fist-full of coals winked in the fire place. The child had cried itself to sleep, its balled fingers tucked under its chin. Granny felt under the covers. "Law, this child is wet and cold," she said. She found a folded napkin that Julie left stacked on a table beside the fireplace in preparation for the child's coming. Beside them were folded several long gowns Julie had sewn of bleached flour sacks. She had stitched pink lace around the sleeves and neck for the coming of her girl child.

It had been foretold in late October that Julie carried a girl baby, the day Margaret Fellers and Olda Wilson came to visit, Olda riding her own child on her hip. Margaret came with a poke of hand-me-downs to loan to Julie for the arrival of her newborn, clothes so tiny it surprised Julie to see them. Boot socks knitted the size of a half-thumb and gowns as long as the half-arm with a draw string at the bottom. "Lord, they outgrow their clothes in a week or two," Margaret said. She had left her four children with her sister for the day.

Julie paraded across the front porch, holding her hands under the suspended full moon of her belly. Olda and Margaret studied Julie's shape. "With a boy child, a woman grows big all over. She'll carry the weight in her back and thighs," said Olda. "This child is carrying in the front," said Margaret. "A girl," they both said. Julie could feel the truth of this in her bones. She had hoped for a girl. She had been an only child, no sisters or mother to talk to. A woman needs to talk to another woman sometimes. But Thomas had ordered a son. "To help with the farming," he said.

Olda and Margaret talked the afternoon of childbirth, of their gripping the headboard in pain, of taking a little gunpowder to ease the birth. They talked of babies born robust, and of stillborns. They passed on their bitter lessons to Julie, the way women must do, telling her she must learn to persevere. "The first one is the hardest because you don't know what you're in for. It's like passing a watermelon. You can hear your bones coming apart," said Olda. She bounced her small boy on her knee and smiled. "You forget the pain soon as the child is born," said Margaret. "Or lord knows, you'd never let a man touch you again."

Olda's baby boy wore a blue knitted bonnet tied under the chin. "You got to keep their head warm," Olda said. "Put a bonnet on your baby for sleeping, too," she said, "to keep the draft off." Julie held Olda's baby for practice. "Boys are the worst for squirming, all arms and legs," said Olda. Margaret brought a square of oil cloth cut from an old tablecloth for Julie to put under the baby's bed clothes. Julie thought what a good ideal for keeping the baby's bed dry.

Julie said she would be nineteen years old come January. "Law, you'd have been an old maid if you'd a waited much longer," Margaret said. "I had my first youngon at fifteen."

"You caught a good man in Thomas Peach," said Olda. "If he's like his daddy, he won't ever be rich, but he'll work."

Julie would not hear of Margaret and Olda leaving without a few jars of blackberry preserves. "Not too many," Margaret said, "It's a burden to carry down the mountain."

Olda turned at the head of the path and called back to Julie who stood on the steps watching them go. "Who's coming to catch the baby?" Olda pulled the blanket tight around her boy. Margaret switched the basket to her other arm.

"I've sent word for Granny Older. If she can make it up the mountain," Julie called to them.

Granny Older pulled the cold, wet napkin off the baby. The quilt was soaked underneath. She said to Thomas, "Warm up the milk. It's in a jar in my basket. Put a pinch of sugar in it."

"Where's Mrs. Finley," said Thomas, only now remembering that Granny Older had gone to fetch her.

"She's down with the mastitis," said Granny. "We'll have to spoon feed the milk, or find us a dropper," she said. "I stopped on by the Kiker farm, and Mace is bringing a cow and her calf up tomorrow."

"I don't have feed for a cow," said Thomas. "No pasture cleared yet. We meant to get us a cow in a year or so."

"Young people get themselves married and never study a whit on what it takes to get through. You're learning the hard way," said Granny.

"I'll walk out tomorrow and find somebody to bring a mule and sled up with a load of hay."

"Julie's daddy is coming with the hay. He's been told," said Granny.

Thomas Peach hated Julie's daddy, and Solomon Moody hated Thomas Peach in the way men do when they fight over the same woman. Julie Moody and Thomas Peach had eloped. In Thomas' way of thinking, Solomon Moody had not intended to give Julie up for marriage, even though she was of age. Solomon took hold of Julie by both arms, and shook her hard, a thing he had never done before. Right there in front of Thomas Peach, right there on the front porch of his home, Solomon said to Julie, "That boy don't have a dime in his pocket. You've not courted six weeks yet. Best to make sure. You got a lifetime to be miserable."

Now Julie was dead.

"If he tries to fault me on Julie's death," Thomas thought, "I'll throw his own doings back at him. His wife died, too, didn't she? The same way as my Julie?" Thomas sorted in his mind what he would say to Solomon when he came, but nothing he thought of came out right in his mind. Solomon Moody could speak a word like an ice pick. He could find a man's fault and plant it back like a burr under the skin.

Thomas searched inside Granny's basket for the jar of milk. The cream, yellow and thick, floated at the top of the jar. "What is this for?" he said, pulling an orange out of the basket and holding it toward Granny Older. He felt the stick of horehound candy in the basket.

"Dorthea sent you some Christmas," Granny said.

Thomas felt anger rise like acid in his throat. "Hell, ain't that a stupid thing to do," said Thomas, "and Julie dead!"

"Dorthea meant well," said Granny. She gave Thomas the hard look she gave to fools.

Granny Older had left Julie's laying out until she could fetch the baby's milk. "Attend to the living," she always said. "The dead will be buried."

Granny meant to heat water for washing the body, but she knew not to say this to Thomas. "Build up a fire in the cook stove," Granny said. "I'll cook us a bite to eat." At the back of the stove was half a skillet of cold cornbread, the last that Julie had baked. Granny sent Thomas to the smokehouse to cut some strips of streaky bacon. She found some dried shucky beans strung on a thread behind the cook stove. She put those in a skillet with water, a piece of meat, and a pinch of sugar. She put on a large pot of clean water to boil on the back eye.

"The potatoes didn't come on good," said Thomas when Granny went looking for some. Granny knew that he had dug the potatoes in the wrong sign. She found them rotted in the cellar, white sprouts growing out of them like the bones of fingers. "There's no potatoes and men coming tomorrow to cook for?" said Granny.

Solomon Moody came with a sled of hay drawn by a mule. Seeing the trees down across the path, he swung wide along the slope of the mountain estimating the lay of the land by the depth of the snow around the tree trunks. He drove the mule and sled against the house where the snow didn't reach. Under the hay he'd laid some tools to build Julie's coffin. The Peach boy didn't likely have a measure or a saw, he knew. He took off his snowy boots when he came inside and left them dripping behind the front door. He stopped first at the crib beside the fireplace to see Julie's baby girl. He studied the child's high forehead and dimpled chin. He smoothed her red hair and saw that it inclined to curl in wisps above her ears. "She takes after my Julie," he said. He was glad not to see Thomas Peach in the child.

Thomas came through the door behind Solomon Moody. "I'm thinking on sending the baby to Evelyn's. I can't be taking care of a baby and trying to work this place," he said.

"You won't be giving Julie's baby to your sister. I'll be taking the baby," said Solomon. "She's come out of my Julie." He looked at Thomas Peach with cold hatred.

Solomon went inside the closed bedroom to where his daughter lay upon the bed. Granny Older had dressed Julie in the dress that Thomas had bought for her Christmas present. Thomas wanted to rail against the old woman for putting the dress on Julie, but he couldn't open his mouth against this hard, scrappy woman. Granny had already cut the dress open behind and wrestled it over Julie's stiff body. He couldn't bear to see her dead in the dress. Her face had lit up like a candled tree at the Birdsong Store when she saw the dress. "I swear to fit in it come spring," she whispered up to Thomas, pressing the dress between her round belly and his belt buckle. Then she held the dress to the front of her and danced. Mrs. Birdsong took Julie aside and whispered at her ear. "Be careful not to fall with another child as soon as this one is born," she said, "or you won't be wearing this dress come spring." Julie's face studied over. She had not thought of this possibility. "Not but one way to do that," Mrs. Birdsong said behind the cup of her hand.

Solomon lifted the white rag soaked in soda water that Granny had laid over Julie's face to keep her from turning dark, but the blood had settled under her eyes. Her lips were black. "That ain't my Julie," Solomon said.

"No," said Granny. "The spirit's flown." Outside, the snow came down heavy and wet.

Solomon went behind the house and jabbed into the planks of the back wall with a crowbar. Some of the boards cracked and split. "Rotten," he said, and tossed them into the snow.

"Laws, Mr. Solomon. What are you doing to my house?" said Thomas. He came out the back door when he heard the boards cracking.

"Julie's box," said Solomon. "I'd a stripped the barn but you ain't built one."

"I mean to build the coffin myself," said Thomas.

"Do you mean to build a coffin with that green chestnut wood?" Solomon said. "Even if you had the time to make planks." Thomas knew that himself, but he'd cut the chestnuts out of anger, a thing he had no way to explain, and now he'd been caught stupid.

When Solomon pulled planks half way up the back of the house, the bedroom wall opened where Julie lay on the bed. The child cried in the next room. Solomon fell to his knees in the snow and wept. Thomas wanted to cry, too, but could not. He gritted his teeth. He felt guilty somehow, but didn't understand why.

"Well, then," said Thomas, "I'll dig the grave. I'm thinking up by that grove there."

"I'm taking Julie down the mountain on the sled," said Solomon. He pulled himself out of the snow.

"Julie's my wife. She's staying up here," said Thomas. He balled up his fists at the ends of his long stiff arms. Solomon Moody wasn't coming up on his mountain and ride over him like a mowing machine.

"You've fixed to give away your own baby, ain't you? That is the same as giving away Julie." Solomon said. He carried the weathered planks and stacked them beside the porch. He looked Thomas square in the eye. "Now then, where are you going to bury the second wife?" He picked up a saw from the snow. This boy didn't even have saw horses. He'd have to lay the planks catty-cornered across the porch rails. "Why do you want to bury your wife on some other man's land anyway?" Solomon said to the boy.

Granny Older came to the back door and slung a dishpan of hot suds across the snow bank. The steam rose like breath from the cold ground. "Get on down the hill," she said to Thomas. "Mace Kiker is struggling a cow and calf up the slope."

Thomas stomped through the snow to the shed and brought out a thin rope.

"Wait until Mace hears there's no need for the cow," said Solomon to Granny Older. "The boy here is fixed to give away Julie's baby to his sister, Evelyn."

Granny's eyes burned on Thomas like hot irons. Thomas was young, but he ought to be tougher, Granny knew.

Thomas shifted in the snow toward Solomon Moody. "I ain't said you can have my baby," Thomas said. He felt his tongue come back into his head. He waded the snow toward Mace. The cow had slid off in a drift, and the calf bawled. He stopped in the snow and came back a few steps. "I'll build a lean-to," said Thomas. "In case you're wondering where I intend to put the cow."

"Well then, me and Mace can help you build it," Solomon said. He went to the shed to find a shovel. "I never seen a man dig a cow out of a snow drift with a rope," he shouted. Thomas half turned and threw up his hand before going back for the shovel.

"Strip some milk from that cow as soon as you can," said Granny. "Supper is a waiting when you get here." She went inside the house. "Laws, men," she said to herself behind the kitchen door, "Barking at each other at a time like this." Granny knew about death, that it brought out the best, and the worst, in people.

Solomon Moody nailed up the lean-to fast. He was not a tall man, but built wide and solid with square jaws and big square hands. Thomas handed him the near rotten planks pulled off the bottom of the house for the frame, and then he sawed the straightest limbs from the felled chestnuts and laid them against the frame in tee-pee fashion. Solomon kept the best planks for Julie's box, laying them straight in a pile under the house eaves. Then he shoveled the snow from under the rough shed and spilled some hay on the muddy ground. Mace laid a burlap sack across the calf's back to keep it warm, and tied her in the lean-to so the cow would follow him. Solomon said that it was odd for a calf to be born this time of the year. He'd only seen a calving at Christmas time once before. The calf found a teat and pulled down hard, then butted.

Solomon Moody raised a piece of hot corn bread across the table, pointing toward Thomas Peach. "I ain't heard you thank Mace for bringing that cow up here," he said. Granny Older came with a hot pot of shucky beans and set it in the middle of the table.

Thomas said, "That's right. You didn't hear me asking for that cow, now did you?"

Granny kicked Thomas's shin under the table with the heel of her heavy boot. She whispered something under her breath that Thomas read upon her lips. He swallowed his food. Directly, he turned and laid his hand on Mace's shoulder. "Thanks to you, Mace. That was a good thing you done," he said.

"We all know to help even when it ain't asked for, nor thanked," Granny said to Solomon. "I'm still waiting on a thank-you myself."

Solomon Moody kept his eyes steady on Thomas Peach. "Don't worry about paying for the use of that cow," he said, knowing that idea had not come to Thomas who wasn't old enough to think ahead to all the details that need attending. Solomon knew that's what keeps a man sane, tending to the small details of everyday life.

The next morning, the snow had stopped. The earth was white and deep. Mace Kiker and Solomon Moody cut some of the chestnuts and stacked wood in a long line against the lee-side of the house. They filled two barrels with cedar kindling, and filled two buckets with snow to melt on the stove to water the cow.

Granny kept Thomas in the house, away from Solomon. "If you mean to keep this baby," she said, "you'd better be learning how to take care of her." Thomas didn't mean to keep the baby, and he didn't mean to give her over to Solomon Moody. He didn't know what he meant to do.

Solomon meant to keep a sharp tongue whittling away at Thomas until the boy fought him. But, not now. Not while Julie lay dead in the cold back room where the snow had drifted through the opened wall. Not while Granny hung about, watching, nor Mace came with the good heart of a neighbor to help out. Not now at Christmas, but in the new year, when the boy was still drowning in his grief and wearied of a crying child. Taking Julie's baby would be easier then. Not now, while the boy was filled with the strength of wild grief. He'd felled eighteen chestnuts in an afternoon.

"I think we ought to settle this right now," said Thomas Peach. He'd pulled off the red shirt, and it lay on the snow like a big drop of blood. His bare chest was pale and glistened where he had sweated anger.

Solomon kept hammering nails into the rough planks he'd pulled off the back of the house. Julie's box, he called it. He'd never have wanted to see Julie buried in this coffin, but he built it to prove to Thomas Peach that he could pull the house right down around him and box his daughter up in that house and haul her down the mountain on his sled. He could show this Peach boy the strength of his quiet hatred. No need to fight now. Solomon turned his back on Thomas and went for another board and another nail. His hammering rung against the hill like a sound of dread.

Thomas came at Solomon from behind, but stopped short when he saw the hammer raised in the air against him. "We'll have this out in the spring," Solomon said. "I'll call on you when the time comes." Then Thomas Peach did a thing that stunted Solomon. Thomas put his hand on the raised hammer so softly that Solomon didn't know what to make of him. "Hit me," Thomas said to Solomon. "Hit me hard. I won't make a move for you. Hit me."

Solomon put the hammer down, turned toward the unfinished box, and picked up a piece of the house lumber he'd pulled off the house the day before. He could hear Thomas sobbing, sobbing hard, somewhere behind him in the snow. He hadn't wanted the boy to let go of his grief. Not yet. He hated to hear the boy sobbing his grief away. Solomon needed the strength of all his anger to carry him through his own grief, and he could feel it melting some.

Solomon finished the coffin in the late afternoon of the second day. He ordered Thomas through the snow toward the open wall where Julie laid dead on her bed. Solomon lifted her at the shoulders and Thomas at the knees, carefully. Thomas thought that Julie felt hard, and heavy like cut wood. She felt solid and unyielding in a way he had not expected. And she was so cold. Granny Older had lined the box with a quilt in the wedding ring pattern of rusty red and dull green colors that Julie had been given as a present after her marriage to Thomas. Mace had put the box onto the sled and brought the mule alongside the opening in the house. The two men passed her through, and Mace caught hold of Julie underneath the small of her back. In a careful way, the three men guided her body into the coffin. Granny Older tucked the quilt around her.

Julie looked dark, almost a bruised dark, against the lightness of the snow outside. Solomon leaned over the box and kissed Julie on the lips, and said farewell. He looked sideways at Thomas as if to say, "See. See who loves Julie the most?" He nailed the lid on the homemade coffin, sending each nail through the wood in one swift throw of the hammer.

Solomon rode the mule and Mace rode the back of the sled down the mountain, the coffin between them. Thomas and Granny stood on the front porch and watched them going down, down through the white mist toward the valley below. The baby girl was asleep inside before the fire. All was quiet except for the sled crunching over the frozen snow and brushing through the trees, and a tingling of church bells so far away.

Some Living Room

Dixon County, Tennessee, 1955

"Time for a serious talk," mother said. "You should know perfectly well by now that a white girl may not visit a Negro in his room." Mother said she would not tell me a second time. She pointed to a hickory switch that she kept on the top of the refrigerator. Mother never chose limber switches, but the thick unbending kind with little knobs protruding. Mother said that I could knock at Silas's door and offer him the dessert that she baked for him each Sunday. I could talk to Silas outside in the light of day. I could even help him gather eggs, or pick apples. After all, he was eighty years old and suffered with arthritis. Nevertheless, Silas Mosely was a Negro, and on no account should I cross his threshold. "People talk about such things," Mother said.

Silas had lived in a shed attached to Mr. John Johnson's barn for nearly thirty years, working for Mr. John and his wife, Irma, for all that time. Mother had known Silas almost as long, and yet I sensed a mysterious fear in her warning about Negroes. I felt inwardly compelled to ignore her warning, partly because I didn't understand her fear, and partly because John and Irma Johnson lived on the hill just above our house. Silas's shed was exactly one hundred steps across the pasture, and a duck under the barbed wire fence. He had always been somewhere in my line of vision, working about the farm or walking down the road toward the river, but as he got older and more feeble, he stayed mostly inside the shed.

Silas never latched the shed door. I rushed headlong into his living quarters nearly every day that I didn't see him outside. Silas might be shelling out green peas, mending horse harness, or sitting at his small table, his head bowed over a plate of pinto beans and onions. "This old nigger man got to sleep with his pants on and take a bath in his clothes, a youngon like you running in. Thank the lord you come hollering. I hear you coming a mile off," Silas often said.

I'd come bounding inside, my hands filled with ferns I had picked in the woods, or a dirt dauber's nest, or a snake's skin, or a row of locust shells burred on my sweater sleeve, or pretty rocks that Silas laid on a shelf, or an enamel doorknob, or a rusted horseshoe, or some yellow flowers that he set in a snuff glass of water on his window ledge. Or, I just came to talk. Silas often fussed about my intrusions. "Youngon, you be coming where white folks ain't allowed."

One Sunday, after the serious talk, mother sent me to Silas's shed with a coconut pie. He met me at the door, but I shot past his long, thin legs, leaving him standing there with his empty hands outstretched toward a mirage of pie.

"Lordy. That youngon like a cat at the door," Silas said. I set the coconut pie daintily on the table, and bounced down on a straight chair, carefully fanning the skirt of my pink crinoline dress across my knees.

"Well, I reckon you going to stay awhile," Silas muttered to himself and shut the door to keep out the flies. Silas went to a broken drawer and brought out a butter knife, picked up two saucers from an open shelf nailed above a cabinet, then sat in the chair at the corner of the table, his long, thin legs squared like two-by-fours in his khaki pants.

"It was good of your mama to send me some pie. I'm going down and tell her my thanks," said Silas. Silas cut two slices of coconut pie, browned and sweet, licked the gum off the ends of his fingers in the way I have seen him rob a bite of honey comb from a bee hive he kept along the edge of the woods, and eat it from his fingertips.

That Sunday afternoon as we were eating the pie, Mr. John came into Silas's shed, opening the wooden door silently. The only sound was the clinking of our forks against our plates. I knew that Mr. John's being inside the shed seemed wrong. Silas's room was his own territory. Mr. John had said himself that he went into Silas's shed for emergencies only, like the time his chicken house caught fire and he needed water buckets. I knew that Mr. John acted peculiar because of the Negro subject that Mama had warned me about.

Silas, to my knowledge, never went beyond Mr. John's porch. I knew this because in summertime when I was not in school and had no one to play with, I sneaked inside the shed in early morning. When the hands of Silas's pocket watch struck 7:00 a.m., he pulled his suspenders over his khaki shirt and walked directly to Mr. John's house.

I witnessed the ritual between Silas and Mr. John on many occasions, Silas standing at the foot of the steps leading to a wide porch where tobacco bed netting kept the fly specks off Irma's white wicker chairs. Mr. John stood at the top of the steps plugging a pipe with tobacco while he talked. Silas mimicked Mr. John's lips and pulled his fingertips to keep track of his jobs. Silas sometimes forget a job on his list, as he did on a Friday morning in the summer of 1954. Silas said, "Youngon, what was that number five job of work?"

I remembered Silas's list, for I had watched intently. I said, pulling my fingertips in Silas's way, "Mr. John says to take Mrs. Tremble's eggs to the store and sell them. She has nearly four dozen in a basket. She's down in her back this week."

Mr. John came inside Silas's shed on the Sunday after Silas had taken the eggs to the store, quietly opening the small door with leather hinges that Silas had fashioned from the tongues of old shoes. There were five or six of these leather tongues nailed up crooked, causing the door to swing lopsided. Silas often said that if everybody in the world had a tongue as quiet as a shoe's, the world would be a better place. Silas had just taken a bite of pie, when suddenly, there stood Mr. John outlined in the Sunday light. Suddenly, we both knew that something was wrong.

Silas scooted back the cane bottomed chair he was sitting on and arose. Besides the meager light from the open door, some dingy light came in through a small window above a cabinet. On the cabinet, the white dots of a speckled enamel pan winked in the scarce light. Mr. John closed the door behind him. In the dimness both Mr. John and Silas wore the same dark faces, the stray light from the window played at the curve of their chins and across their teeth.

At first Silas seemed agitated, and then he seemed confused. He shifted his feet toward Mr. John, his blind hand felt for something solid to steady him. I could hear the words come quietly out of Silas's mouth, "What on earth?" Silas's breath hitched in his chest, the words caught like dry bread in his throat. When Silas tried to speak again, his quivering lips could not form words.

Mr. John walked several steps inside the shed, all the time kneading the brim of his hat. He did not speak directly, but looked about the shed. His eyes fell upon the horse collar hanging on the wall above

Silas's cot, a hoe and a mattock in a corner, the sagging cot where Silas slept, his blankets neatly tucked under the mattress, and a small coal stove that Silas cooked on during the summer months as well. The room always stayed too warm and smelled like a potter's oven. The constant heat had cooked the red clay floor stone hard. Silas swept the earth floor with shocks of broom sage which he grew in the sass patch beyond the barn. Mr. John's eyes took in everything, even the cracked cup on a plank ledge below the window where Silas soaked his dentures with a drop or two of bleach.

Finally, he spied the table where I sat before my piece of coconut pie. Mr. John gave me only a passing glance, but since I feared he would send me home, I said, "My mother sent up some coconut pie for Silas and me to eat. My mother won't mind if you have a piece, too." Mr. John seemed not to hear me at all, but turned and spoke directly to Silas whose long, lean body waved like a willow limb in the dim light.

"Did you give Mrs. Tremble her egg money Friday?"

"Yes sir." Silas felt inside his pants pockets. He drew up some change in the well of his hand, held it to the window, and raked the coins with his fingers. "This here is my money. I toted Missus Tremble's egg money in my left pocket." Silas patted his empty pocket.

"I talked to Mrs. Tremble at church today," said Mr. John. "Mrs. Tremble says she sent four dozen eggs to the store, and you didn't bring back all of her money."

"Yes, Mr. John," said Silas. "Missus Birdsong over at the store candled them eggs. She said some of them eggs be rotten and some of them eggs be pippin."

"Why didn't you bring the pippin eggs back and put them under the setting hen?"

"Well, that Missus Birdsong throwed them eggs to her dogs."

"You got a tongue in your head. Why didn't you ask her for the eggs back?"

"I standing on the front porch. She throwed them eggs out the back door. Missus Birdsong says I better not brang no rotten eggs to her store."

"Why didn't you tell Mrs. Birdsong the eggs came from Mrs. Tremble?"

"Well, Mr. John. I reckon I didn't think on it that way."

"Mrs. Tremble's an old lady. She thinks you've done something wrong. She thinks she's owed some money. We'll have to work something out about paying that back."

After Mr. John left the shed, Silas sat down on the edge of his cot. His face drew up like a string purse.

"My mother will go and talk to Mrs. Birdsong," I said. "She'll pay that egg money back."

"Lord, no. Don't you be mouthing a thing to Missus Birdsong. Lord no," said Silas.

I never knew how Mr. John and Silas worked out Mrs. Tremble's egg money, just that afterwards Silas seemed upset, his face always pinched up in thought.

One fatal day late that summer I went inside Silas's shed to show him a big bullfrog that I had trapped beside the pond in my dress tail. Silas was uninterested in the biggest bullfrog on earth, and particularly its loud croaking. Not to be ignored, I turned the bullfrog loose on Silas's table, and it jumped smack into a pot of chicken and dumplings that had just come boiling off the stove. We hovered over the steaming pot studying the bullfrog as it struggled in the hell broth. Silas said if he'd wanted frog legs he'd have fried him some. He gigged the limp frog out of the gravy with his fork, and pitched it out the open door. "Let the dogs have at it," he said. "I'm having some chicken."

"I'm going to catch another frog," I said, "A bigger one." Silas mumbled something as I left.

I saw my mother coming up the hill, brandishing her hickory switch. She had been sitting on our front porch talking to Irma, and caught sight of my red gingham dress fluttering out the shed door. Mother said I might as well have been waving a flag at her. The switch stung my legs so bad my eyes watered up, but I refused to cry.

I never visited Silas Mosely in his shed after that day. I was even too afraid to speak to him. I did see him from time to time, away on the hill, hunched over his garden patch, or walking from the barn with a bucket of milk, or disappearing into the apple orchard above Irma's hen house.

Silas died in his sleep during the early spring of 1955. I watched from our front yard as several Negro men carried Silas to a hearse.

Silas lay on the stretcher under a white sheet, the bumpy outline of his head, his crossed arms, his feet protruding underneath, and seeing the three Negro men dressed in white shirts and dark suits, carrying him to the hearse made the whole world seem quiet and invisible.

Mama said to come inside out of the cold, and to stop staring at people. That was not polite. Later, I seemed to remember the Forsythia was budding. There might have been some patches of snow in the shadow of the hill. Much later, it occurred to me that John and Irma Johnson were watching the Negroes from behind the porch railing at the same spot where Silas sometimes sat on the porch and watched the *Amos and Andy* show through the side window.

A few weeks after Silas died, Mr. John tore down the shed and burned the planks in the open pasture. Afterwards, he plowed up the hard red earth with much difficulty, and Irma planted a lettuce bed in the shade of the barn. Mama declared that it was foolish to plant anything in that hard clay dirt, fallow for so many years. What on earth were John and Irma thinking? Nothing could grow there. Not ever.

Rock Big and Sing Loud

When Orey Banks reached the summer of her 106th year, she took the notion to die. That summer she felt a strange sadness, something lost that she could never get back, something she could not name. "I am old," she thought to herself. "Why ain't I dead?" Old man death must have got into the house when she was not paying attention, but on the particular day when he came to her consciously, she didn't even fetch in a bucket of water from the cistern. She propped the broom in the corner. She shooed the cats toward the barn and ordered them to fend for themselves. Hadn't she let the summer garden go to weeds, the lawn grow over with Queen Anne's lace that bobbed like the heads of grey-haired old women in green dresses? Through the kitchen window the Queen Anne's nodded, yes, yes. Orey let slip from her hands the old habits of a century that now seemed vastly unimportant, even silly. "Let the hens sit on their eggs," she thought, knowing the basket sat empty by the back door. "Let the eggs rot. Or let them hatch. No matter."

It was the comfortable love she felt in her little house that kept her living. This was the house her father built with a stone foundation, yellow Poplar planks, and a roof of copper half an inch thick. The house hadn't leaked a drop in the hundred years Orey had lived there. Orey also had twenty-six acres of land to walk on, and stand in the sunshine. It was the house and the land that kept her alive. Orey knew that to die she must lock herself out of the house. Her house hadn't been locked in half a century, not since her mother and father had passed, not since her children had grown up and died, not since her husband, Sam Banks, was still living. Orey had a time finding the big master key, the kind that locks dungeons, taped behind a chest of drawers, the place her husband had hidden it for safe keeping. Finding the key made Orey think of her husband, Sam, a man who never turned a hand to work, yet saved every useless thing as if it were gold, even the scraps of string too short to tie. She found the matchbox of string he'd saved under the bed with a family of newborn mice, still blind and pink struggling among the threads. She tossed them into the fire under the stove eye. Everything Sam Banks had ever done collected dust and vermin, she thought. She was glad he was dead.

Orey snicked the latch of the backdoor from the inside. She planned to go out the front door and lock that behind her with the dungeon key. Before that, she gazed around for the last time at the home where she had raised thirteen children, bedding them on pallets and shuck mattresses. At night the children were wedged together in the few small rooms like quilt squares. The bedrooms were empty now except for her mama's big tall bed against the living room wall. Orey, who was four feet and eleven inches, and too shriveled and humped to climb into the bed, slept instead on a horsehair sofa in her tiny parlor, low and soft, she'd kept covered all the years her children were growing up. The only nice piece of furniture she owned. "Now look what I've come to. Sleeping on my good couch and not minding a hill of beans about wearing it out."

Orey toured the palace of her mind with her fingers reading the Braille of the fireplace. She laid her hands atop fifty years of fireplace soot that had settled thickly on the chimney stones. Orey's blue eyes bleached with age couldn't really see the pictures on the fireplace clearly. She saw from the inward eye of memory her family bunched together on the mantle, on a square oak table beside a window, pictures propped here and there, her only company for these many years. She picked up each one and saw her child's face, a habit of memory snapped clearly inside her brain, for the faces in the photographs had nearly gone white in the sun. Her feet knew from habit where to walk and her hands knew where to reach for each picture.

"Lord a mercy, look what a young husband my Sam was," she rubbed his face with the ball of her thumb. "Burn in hell, Sam. You rascal. I'm heading in the other direction," she said to her dead husband. She laughed hard and deep when she thought of Sam Banks dead and burning in hell.

Orey scooped the pictures off the table, pulled some out of the top drawer and bundled the whole mess in her apron. She marched out the front door, down the front steps, to the cistern. "My babies' pictures ain't nobody's business but mine," she said, scooting the iron lid off the cistern and dropping her family, one at a time, through the bucket hole and down, down into the cold water.

Orey said her farewells. Soon she would join her family in the strange country called death. She was sure they would be there to meet her, smiling. It would be like a reunion, so much better than living forever and alone as she seemed now to be doing. Orey kissed the photographs one at a time, before she sent them floating down the cistern. "Good bye, Elizabeth, my youngest. Sam, Junior, not a thing like your daddy, thank God. Elsie Joan, my oldest, and my best help, goodbye. Lester, you ran off. Maybe you ain't dead yet. Buckley, my no-goodest one, I hope you made it to heaven anyway, although I have doubts. Prissy Jean, my smartest one, goodbye. Axel, my quiet one, and Ruth, my funniest one. Goodbye. When I get blue-down, I still hear you laughing in the wind. Louis, my serious one, my oldest boy. Dead in the war. Goodbye. You're the only one I didn't see buried, Louis. Here's a kiss for you. And here is Jacob, named after your granddaddy. In you go, my kindest child. I'll never forget you bringing me flowers in a jelly glass, and you so cripped in the joints. Hobart, my last child dead and gone these six years. I meant to die before you, Hobart. Well, this one I can't remember, but I will study awhile and your name will come. Goodbye, anyway. And my deary little Gladys, dead in my arms at three years, your picture is in the well of my heart."

Down the pieces of faded paper floated. Now she wouldn't have to turn the pictures to the wall as one does after a death in the house. She thought to cover the mirrors inside the house with black cloth, but couldn't remember if she still had a mirror. She hadn't looked at herself in years. When had she last combed her hair? She must look a fright, she thought. "Never mind," Orey screeched the metal lid back across the cistern-hole. Now, that part of her plan was finished.

Orey saved Sam's picture for last. "Now, Sam, you old heathen. I'm going to burn you with a match." She drew out a box of matches she carried always in her apron pocket, and lit a flame to the stiff card of her husband's face. He curled dark and wispy, then flaked away. "I should have burned you years ago," Orey said to herself after Sam's face was gone. "Gone from my heart. Gone from my mind." Orey laughed so hard that her small belly moved up and down under her apron.

Orey took the feed store calendar, 1982, off the wall and wrote her testament on the clean back pages, feeling the edges of the paper between her fingers and the point of a stub pencil.

I, Orey Banks, have a right sound body for 106 years of age, except for a bad hip joint and a bit of arthritis in my left knee. I still know a hack from a handsaw, so I reckon my mind is going well enough. Although I doubt my eyes on some occasions, especially the day I saw Sam walking about in my garden looking over my tomato plants and him dead 30 years. I set my old yard dog, Trucker, on him that is also dead now, and yet he came to chase Sam away. And there was other times, too, like the boy I saw in the tree handing me a bowl of strawberries.

Anyway, I will not be shut away in the Asbury Methodist Home for the extreme elderly, as I visited that place on my 100th birthday for the oct-to-gonary party, and they are old people who don't have nary a brain left in their heads. Now, how am I going to talk to them people? I will not be shut up. And I will not eat Beulah Simmons nasty cooking, for I seen her wipe her nose on her apron. Lord, lord. I have no strength left to plant and hoe my garden, nor can my vegetables, nor have my own fire to set by and so forth and so on. So I have asked the Lord God who has granted me the favor of outliving my sorry husband, Sam Banks, to take me to heaven on August 12 of this year, for that is my birthday and I ain't got no living relatives nearby, and my grandchildren never say so much as hidey-ho, so I give my home seat to the Dixon County Poor Farm for folks that ain't never had a peaceful place to lay their heads. My own mama went there to live after Sam put her out of the house, and her such a help to me and my little ones, only because she didn't like his cussing and drinking and laziness and how he beat us now and then.

And if a body reads this and thinks it is the ideals of a dumb woman or a crazy woman, just say to them that I would have starved and froze to death long before now if my head wasn't on right. And that is proof. I am running out of calendar. Don't let them good for nothing grandchildren have a thing and I will go to heaven a happy woman. Signed. Orey Margaret Preston Banks. I hope I have not writ over my own words too much as my fingers are feeling where to write. Thank you.

Orey rolled up her testament and tucked it inside the screen door where it wouldn't blow away, and then she went back to the cistern and dropped the key down the bucket hole.

Orey decided to die on her front porch in her rocking chair where she had spent many a pleasant moment alone. "Well, I've been alone most of my life, I might as well die alone."

Since hardly a soul came to visit Orey, she thought it perfectly safe to plan her dying day according to her own whims. She imagined the home health nurse, Ruth Rutherford, who came weekly for Orey's checkup, would be the one to find her dead body, a question mark too stiff to un-curve from the old rocker. "Let them carry me off and bury me in this rocker." She laughed at this vision of herself dead, dried flat and green as a frog in the road, and Nurse Ruth finding her in such a predicament.

Nurse Ruth Rutherford came to Orey's home, high atop the hilly farm, in her four-wheel drive, religiously. "Give me your left arm, Miss Orey, and let me check that blood pressure." The nurse wrapped the blood pressure cuff around several times. "Lord, Miss Orey, your arm is no bigger than a broom handle. 110 over 90."

"That's the same as it's always been," says Orey. "You don't need to tell me that."

Nurse Ruth peered in Orey's ears with a pointed flashlight. "I don't see any birds in there," says Nurse Ruth, trying to amuse Orey Banks, who was not easily amused.

"One of these days I hope you find a big barn owl back in my head and then you'll be satisfied, I reckon," says Orey, and the nurse laughs, and says, "Miss Orey, you are a sight."

"That owl ain't going to like having a lantern shined back in his dark hole, and he's going to come fluttering his big wings right in your face before you can get out of the way."

"Lord, Miss Orey, you are a sight."

"A flogging by that big owl will serve you right, Nursey-girl."

"What a sight you are, Miss Orey. Now open your mouth wide. Ahhhhhhhaaaa. That's good. Your throat looks fine. Now let me shine the light up your nose, Miss Orey."

"Don't wake up them bats, Nursey-girl. They'll pelt you like hail stones raining crossways."

Orey didn't like meddling, and Nurse Ruth was a meddler. Nurse Ruth had reported Orey Banks' remarkable longevity to the Geriatrics Research at the East Tennessee State University's Quillen Medical School. "The doctors want to study your genetic makeup, Miss Orey, see what makes you spry as a cricket."

"What they going to do to study my genetic?" The corners of Orey's mouth drew down.

"Well," says Nurse Ruth, "they'll likely examine you from head to toe, and then they'll draw some blood and run tests."

"What makes you think I got extra blood for giving away? And I ain't going to let a bunch of men poke at me. No sir, not on this old body."

Orey thought that was the end of that, but one day she was standing in the garden picking beetles off her green peppers, mashing them between her thumb and fingers and dropping them in an apron pocket when she heard the awfullest noise coming up the holler. The grinding sounds ricocheted off the walls of the mountains and hammered her ears which were a touch deaf. She poked over to the edge of the hill and watched the procession of four wheel drive vehicles growling up the steep slope to her house.

"Lord have mercy. What is this a-coming?"

When they arrived at the top of the hill, a bunch of young people, men and women, rolled out of the procession toting equipment and bags. One man carried a video camera. Then Nurse Ruth Rutherford came around a Jeep. "These are students from the Med School come to see you, Miss Orey."

Orey tottled up to the porch and picked up a piece of stove wood. "I ain't going to pee in that little bottle. I ain't going to be examined. I'll answer one or two of them questions you want to ask, but that is all, or I'll lay this piece of stove wood against somebody's hide." She waved a stick of wood weakly in her right hand.

All Orey Banks had to say into the young man's video camera was that a good plug of chewing tobacco every day and you'll live a long life. Orey pulled out her lower lip and showed them her chewing tobacco nestled like a dark egg inside her cheek. "I can hold it in there all day and never have to spit much a-tall. And I don't abide them nasty spit cans. You got to spit out on the ground. Watch this young man," Orey worked up the spit on the edge of her tongue, pursed her old lips and let a streak of tobacco juice strike the porch post where the wisteria climbed.

"Folks say I can spit on a dime twenty yards away." Orey pursed her lips toward the camera and the young man danced back into a clump of weeds, the streak of juice whizzing past his ear.

"You are a sight, Miss Orey," said Nurse Ruth, motioning everyone back into their all-terrain vehicles. "I'll be up to see you again next week."

The procession of vehicles turned around in the grass near the barn and grumbled back down the hill. Orey called after them shaking her stick in the air. "You ain't going to cut on me after I'm dead, neither, so don't get your hopes up on that one. I ain't signing no papers to be cut on."

Orey imagined herself dead, stretched out on a table and all the young medical students standing over her with thin stainless knives. They'd be sorry they cut on her. Her guts would turn into long snakes and they would strike out with poison fangs. Her lungs would puff up like bullfrogs, bellowing awful sounds. All of her body parts would turn to something ugly and rebel in the most frightful way. That would teach them not to cut on Orey Banks!

"But never mind that," she thought. "I'm still alive is the problem. It's the good Lord above done made me live this long. But now, He's gone overboard and I'm going to be stuck here on earth forever."

She got to thinking, "Has it been a week a-ready since them doctor-fellers was here? It'd be my luck to get fixed to die and that meddlesome Nursey-girl might come to take my blood pressure."

Orey planted herself into the rocking chair on the front porch, pulled up her ankle socks and smoothed out her apron. She dangled her feet above the porch floor like a little girl. "Might as well go out comfortable," she whispered to herself. Orey gazed out at the fields and the trees rattling in the summer wind, the flowers drooping moist blooms in the early morning, her favorite time, when the mist is rising off the valleys and lifting like a bridal veil to the beautiful faces of flowers. Death will come this way, the veil rising and there will be heaven. Suddenly, a stiff breeze came in gusts and rocked Orey back and forth. She dozed off, the morning sun streaming on her face, the red sky budding cloud-rosettes.

The wind shook Orey and she mumbled in her sleep, "Is somebody there? I'm not going on with you. You're dead. I'm not going over with no dead person. I want to see Jesus coming up my path like he does on the church fans, the ones with the stick handles. Oh, Jesus, you can come knocking on the door. I like that fan, too. But I ain't going with you," Orey mumbled aloud, and her eyes closed and dreaming. "You ain't got no lamb in the crook of your arm. No staff either. Where you taking me," Orey put out her arms and fought the air. "That way don't look right. I'll get my stick on you!" Orey couldn't make out the face coming at her from the hill above the house.

"Daddy. Daddy," Orey cried. "Daddy come and get me. I'm afraid." Orey Bank's daddy came rustling through the corn, old and bent over. He was smiling and his face shone brightly. He came up the path walking, his feet not touching solid ground. "I've come to take you home, Orey Banks," he said. Like the twinkling of an eye, Orey's daddy sat in the rocking chair and old Orey Banks was a child again sitting in her daddy's lap. She smelled the wood smoke smell of his work clothes and the faint scent of sweat and the fried bacon breakfast smell of his breath. Her daddy fried his bacon on the tongs of a fork over the coals in the fireplace. He caught the drips in a saucer and Orey sopped the grease with bread.

Orey felt two places at once, the beginning of her life, and the end, and her life came together like the ends of a soft ribbon, and bow-tied. But surely she must be young again. She knew the stubble of her father's beard, and saw the familiar line of dirt under his fingernails that never could be scrubbed out with soap, or scratched out with his pocketknife.

"Don't we have to walk somewhere, Daddy, like Jesus taking us down some path?"

"We can go right here in this big rocking chair," her daddy said. He pulled the tail of his sweater around her goose-bump legs, and felt Orey trembling like a frightened bird, the way she did when she was cold. He knew the way to sooth Orey, the child, when she was fretful in the night, and nothing could be done but rock and rock. "Rock big, Daddy," said Orey the child. "Rock big and sing loud." The voice of an old familiar hymn sounded against the mountain, and Orey slept.

Dying was just like rocking back in time. Rocking, rocking back until her memory was not bigger than a shoebox. No. It was a cigar box. Orey had buried her first dead newborn in a cigar box. The box was real pretty with a girl painted on the front, dark the way her baby girl might have looked had it lived longer than one night on earth. Orey called the girl Caramelo after a sweet candy someone had given her once for Christmas.

"Now, what kind of name is Caramelo," said the woman looking over Orey as she put the last bit of dirt over her child's shallow grave. It was Orey's old snippy mother-in-law talking to her. "We watched you doing it," said Orey's mother-in-law, who blessedly fell dead of a burst blood vessel while cussing out the apple tree salesman the year after Orey and Sam married. "There ain't no secrets here you know. Now get on down that path," said the old crone mother-in-law. "Pick up them twigs for kindling." She pointed to sticks along the strange path that wound under the shadows of trees.

"What for?" said Orey.

"You know what for," said the crone who looked like a dried prune, black and awful. She had a hickory switch in her hand and lashed it across Orey's back.

"But the baby come too soon," said Orey. She studied the woman, and didn't see a halo. "I ain't going nowhere with you," Orey shouted. The dead mother-in-law grabbed Orey by the wrist and dug her sharp nails in Orey's weak flesh." Orey cried out, "Oh, Jesus. Oh, Jesus," and the sticks flew out of her arms and turned into straw on the wind, and Orey was back at the edge of the path, her father across the yard, rocking gently on the porch.

Orey thought to run to the porch, to run to her daddy's arms where she would be safe again, but her own dead mother stepped between her and the father who was still rocking, and waiting. Her mother was dressed in a thin nightgown. She had not laid eyes on her mother since the day she had put her clothes in a pillowcase and walked away, down the dusty road.

"You let that awful man of yours throw me to the poor house. Out of my own home. I was good enough to share what I had with you and your children and that lazy man of yours. What did I get? My last years spent at the poor farm. You didn't even come to my laying away.

I had nary a soul to see me off but the man who dug the grave, and I can't even tell you his name." The old dead mother was weeping on the sleeve of her nightgown.

"I had seven babies—no mama, I had eight little ones tugging my dress tail when that minister came to tell me you was dead and buried, all the way across the other side of Dixon County.

"And I ain't got a head stone. My name ain't writ where people can read me, and no flowers on my plot. They've done forgot I'm there." Orey saw a deep fire of sorrow burning in her mother's eyes, and a sunken place in the ground where her mother's feet should be. "You're a merry one, Orey Banks, thinking you can decide your day of departure. I wanted awful bad to be laid to bed with your daddy over there. You always got your rocking, one way or the other," her mother said. "And what did I get?"

"Oh, Jesus," prayed Orey, "Take me away from my good old mama. I should have walked with my children to her grave," she said.

The very second she said the word children, each and every one of Orey Bank's children, all toddling age, lined up in a row between her father in the rocking chair and her. "Rock me, Mama," they all cried at once. "Rock me. Rock me," their arms stretched to be picked up. So many at one time. The children were crying. Some of them had a runny nose. They seemed cold as winter. But wasn't it still August? They had all been in the dirt playing. Orey's first instinct was to put them in the horse trough and wash their dirty hands and faces, and then make a big pan of cornbread. She'd never seen so many hungry, dirty children at once needing her rocking arms, and not time to rock them one at a time, let alone all at once. A great weight of dread came upon her. "This must be hell. I got to feed, wash, and rock all my children to the end of time." Eternity stretched out before her like a never-ending line of dirty, crying children.

Orey picked up a dirt clod and threw it toward her children. "All of you scat off. I'm done through with every one of you children. You're all dead and buried. I ain't rocking nary a one." Orey threw dirt clods from the dusty yard at all of her dead children until they fled away crying.

"Now, Orey Banks, you get a hold of yourself," a voice behind Orey said. "You've got to figure out what's real in this world and what's not. It's your past catching up with you," the voice said. "Now you come on with me. I can show you where to get a good time." The voice was that of a woman, young and busty, in a tight red dress hitched way up to her rear end, and no underwear on, but when she smiled she had teeth like Indian corn, nine different colors. Her face was covered in the pox.

"Don't you recognize me?" said the voice. Orey leveled her hand above her eyes and squinted. It was her husband's youngest sister, the one who died of the syphilis. Her name was Sophie. "What you want to have all them youngons for?" said Sophie. "They ain't no fun in that."

Orey bit her tongue, but Sophie knew what Orey wouldn't say. "You ain't no different than me, Orey Banks. You liked a man in your bed as well as the next woman."

Orey spoke back. "I don't want forty-eleven men, though. One man did me just fine. And now I must be dead, I sure don't want no man alive," said Orey to the voice in the red dress who walked toward the porch, the rocking chair, who had her red eyes fixed on Orey's daddy.

"Who wants a man alive?" said Sophie. "I'm going to take you to the man-place where you do it all the time, where you never swell and you never tell."

The sweet and acrid scents of perfume and sulfur burned Orey's nose. She reached in her pocket for the white lace handkerchief to cover her face, but what she pulled out was the box of matches. "You always was a hussy," said Orey. "You died of the pox. You still got the sores."

"And you was carrying a child when you married my brother, Sam. And that baby you buried in the night in that little box, you got by some other man. And don't you lie to me. Your life is all writ down. Now your lie is writ down, too. You never told my brother, did you?"

There came the sound of an ax chopping at the woodpile. Orey looked beyond to where her husband, Sam, brought his ax down on a chunk of stove wood. He wore his funeral clothes, the brown suit someone had given Orey for his decent burial, and there was the fool, out chopping wood. He didn't have sense to change his clothes before doing his work, Orey started to tell him. Sam Banks threw several chunks of wood on the pile. Orey thought that he had never cut that much wood in his life, but the wood was stacked higher than her husband's head. "Orey, I cut the wood for you," he grinned that big white toothy grin that made Orey love him. Or, maybe, she thought, it was lust after all.

"Ask her about the baby," Sophie said to Orey's husband.

"I've read the big book that talks about the baby that wasn't mine," Sam said to Orey.

"Why, you never learned to read," said Orey. "What book?"

"The book of your life," said Sophie, shaking her hips.

"What business of yours to be reading in my book?" said Orey.

"That book talked out loud to me," said her husband, "and showed me the pictures of your doings. You've gypped me, Orey, and I've come to take you."

"I wouldn't go on a cake walk with you, Sam Banks, let alone to hell." Orey pulled out the matches and struck one after the other. She set fire to the wood pile. She threw sticks of burning wood. "I ain't going yet, not going anywhere with you." Orey felt hot and sweaty. "You go back to hell where you came from," screamed Orey. She felt her voice far away bouncing off the hills. The stack of stove wood was almost gone, and Sophie and the husband were trying to come at her through the flames. Then her children came and huddled around their dead grandmother. Then the dead baby, Caramelo, came with the cigar box in her hand. Orey felt each stick of wood heavier than the last, and nearly gone. "I ain't going with you. You can't make Orey Banks go to hell."

"Orey Banks, you are a sight," said Nurse Ruth, holding Orey's flashing hand and deciding whether to tie her wrists to the bed again for her own protection. Nurse Ruth waved salts under Orey's nose and knew that she was finally coming around.

"I ain't going nowhere," said Orey Banks. "You just get out of my yard and go home."

Orey thought she heard the voice of the Nursey-girl saying, "Lord, Miss Orey, you are a sight."

"Are you dead, too?" said Orey. "I've got a stick or two of fire wood here. I'll lay it up side your head if you don't turn me loose right this minute. I ain't going nowhere with you. Hear me!"

Nurse Ruth untied one of Orey's wrists and laid her fingers against the thin veins. "Oh, Jesus, Jesus," screamed Orey.

"Miss Orey, you are a sight!" said Nurse Ruth Rutherford. "You know I wouldn't hurt you."

Orey could feel her own blood pulsing lightly under the nurse's fingers, and then she felt the rocking of her own heart inside the cave of her chest, and she heard her daddy's voice singing somewhere far off, and then it was finished.

About the Author

Tamara Mashburn Baxter was born in Greeneville, Tennessee, and grew up on Pumpkin Bloom Farm situated on the Nolichucky River in Greene County. During her childhood, she traveled a great deal on the river, across the backwoods areas, and around her rural farming community, which centered at the crossroads of New Ebenezer Presbyterian Church, Walker's Elementary School, and Susong's Country Store, a place that inspired many of her earlier works. When she was seventeen, she moved to

Tamara Baxter

Greeneville, and later she moved to Johnson City, Tennessee, and attended East Tennessee State University.

During her college years, Baxter began her writing career. Her first short story, "The Curing," was published by Albert Stewart in *The Appalachian Heritage*. She completed her master's thesis with a collection of stories titled *Pennies Kill the Fishes, and Other Stories*. Baxter continued her studies in fiction with mentors such as Lee Smith, Robert Morgan, Gurney Norman, and Lisa Alther. Her stories, both comic and tragic, take place in the rural and small town settings of Southern Appalachia, and focus on the relationships between parent and child, husband and wife, the individual and the land, the individual and the community, and on what may occur during the narrow slip of time between life and death.

She currently lives in Kingsport, Tennessee, with her husband and teaches literature and writing at Northeast State Community College in Blountville, Tennessee.